BENNY

JPB COLFER

Colfer, Eoin

Benny and Omar

For Jackie

Thank you to May Meyler,
Jean Hersrud, and June Cottgrove

AUTHOR'S NOTE

The Arabic used in this book is Tunisian street slang
and may not conform to standard Arabic spelling or pronunciation.

Text copyright © 1998 by Eoin Colfer

For information address Hyperion Books for Children,
114 Fifth Avenue, New York, New York 10011-5690.

Originally published in Ireland by The O'Brien Press Ltd.
Reprinted by permission.
First Hyperion Paperbacks edition, 2007
1 3 5 7 9 10 8 6 4 2
Printed in the United States of America
Library of Congress Cataloging-in-Data on file.
ISBN-13: 978-1-4231-0282-3
ISBN-10: 1-4231-0282-7

Visit www.hyperionbooksforchildren.com

ALSO BY EOIN COLFER:

Benny and Babe

The Artemis Fowl series

The Wish List

The Supernaturalist

Eoin Colfer's Legend of Spud Murphy

Eoin Colfer's Legend of Captain Crow's Teeth

Eoin Colfer's Legend of the Worst Boy in the World

Half Moon Investigations

CONTENTS

1

WHERE?

Benny Shaw was built like a ferret, or so Father Barty liked to tell everybody. Short and skinny with bandy legs you could roll a basketball through. At this moment his brow was wrinkled in concentration.

The two goalposts looked like there was only half an inch between them. And there was a whole shower of grunting, hairy fullbacks just itching for him to make a mess of the shot. The pressure was well and truly on. Not just any old puck-about: this was the Primary Schools County Hurling Final. St. Jerome's of Wexford facing the Christian Brothers of Wexford. Deadly serious.

Father Barty Finn was at Benny's shoulder, muttering advice, a cigarette jiggling in his false teeth. Barty coached each game like he was standing beside Pearse in the GPO. Schoolwork was grand, but hurling was sacred.

"Take your point, boy," hissed Barty.

Sound advice. They were already in injury time. A point

would square it. No need to risk losing everything by going for a goal. Buy a replay. Even at that, it was a knacky shot.

A sideline, ten yards out. You'd have to really get under a ball to lift it at this range. Benny could try lobbing it in to one of his teammates, but the marking was tight. Fierce-faced little terriers clashed hips, waiting for the ball to drop in the square in front of the goal.

Benny concentrated on the sliotar, the small leather ball before him. He stooped low and sliced his hurley beneath it. It was a sweet shot. He knew it the instant he hit it. No flat jarring up the handle of the hurley, and barely a blade of grass pulled out of the muck.

The sliotar arced high, loaded with backspin, buzzing above the hurley range of the defenders. Benny glared after his shot, sweet-talking it into the square. The players lowered their hurleys. It was out of their control now. The trajectory looked a bit off, but there was a bend on it, dragging the sliotar across the face of the goal. Too late, the keeper, who was already eating a victory burger in his head, realized the danger. He whipped up his hurley, but the bullet had already gone past.

A goal! St. Jerome's was two points ahead. No way back for the Brothers. The park erupted. Parents danced on the benches. Schoolboys howled derision at the opposite stand. As Father Barty often said: *It's not the winning that matters, it's beating the other chaps.*

The Brothers tried a quick puck-off to gain time, but the ref blew it up. All over. Benny pulled off his helmet just in time for Father Barty to tip ash all over his head.

"Good lad, Shaw," he cackled. "That'll learn those chancers."

Benny wore the medal inside his vest. It knocked against his ribs as he ran home, reminding him of the goal. The kiddies were on the path playing kerbsie. George was there being cute. His favorite trick. Benny scowled. Just the sight of his little brother darkened his mood. Nine was too old for cute. Ma had him this way—Jessica Shaw's little actor, swathed in designer outfits. George actually cared about clothes. This was incomprehensible to Benny, who rarely arrived home without a few extra holes in his pants.

And George actually liked drama. He thought acting in pageants and plays was important. What was the point in pretending to be someone else when everyone knew who you were anyway? Benny didn't see the attraction. And pictures? Why would anyone sit inside drawing some old tree when you could be outside climbing up one?

"Mother's looking for you," his brother shouted at him.

Benny grunted. Imagine calling your Ma "Mother." It felt wrong in his mouth, like when you crammed a whole digestive biscuit into your gob and it hit the back of your throat. That was Jessica Shaw—always different. There was the whole name thing, for example. George and Bernard Shaw, after some old fellow who wrote plays. And she always called him Bernard, except when she was annoyed and forgot to stand on ceremony. Then it was "Benny," in tones that would freeze mercury.

The car was by the gate. Da must be home from work. Time for a daily ritual. Benny hopped up on the wall, landing neatly on his own ingrained footprints. There was a side door between the wall and garage, gloss green with a cracked and peeling center. Benny let fly. The sliotar sped to its target, knocking off a few more paint chips. But the latch held. This one was surviving longer than the others. Possibly Da had rigged it, just to annoy him. Might have to do a bit of midnight screw-driving.

Pat Shaw appeared at the porch. He gave Benny the obligatory glare for whacking the door, but he couldn't hold it.

"Well?" He looked like he was waiting for hospital-test results.

Benny raised his medal by the ribbon.

"Good man," Da said, breaking into a relieved grin. "Here, show me that slab of gold."

The two Shaws came together awkwardly, both grinning like eejits. Pat chanced a hug, throwing an arm around his boy. It was more like a headlock, but Benny got the idea.

"What score did you get?"

Benny calculated. "Two goals, four points."

"Out of how much?"

"Two-eleven."

Pat nodded. "So what happened to the other seven?"

Benny croaked out a laugh. "So, how come you're home?"

His father's humor faded suddenly. "Well, Bernard . . . that is, Benny . . . we have to talk. It's important."

"I never touched him."

"No, no. God, I wish that was all."

A voice floated through the hall. "Patrick? Is it our eldest?"

"Let's show your mother this medal," said Pat Shaw, his large hand wrapped fondly around his son's skull.

Jessica Shaw wore a lot of masks. Two silver ones on a pendant. A couple more on hand-painted ceramic earrings, and a gold brooch with four tiny cubic zirconia eyes. She collected them. Apparently the smiley chap and frowning lad represented the yin and yang of the dramatic arts. Benny had made the blunder of asking about that once. Jessica had given him a fifteen-minute lecture contrasting some characters called Falstaff and Ophelia. It was all very educational: Benny learned not to ask any more questions about drama.

Following his dad into the kitchen, Benny lobbed his kit into the black hole underneath the stairs. His mother was seated at the table, a steaming cup of coffee before her. Inevitably, the drama masks were etched into the hand-cast mug. At least Jessica was easy to shop for. George, the little crawler, managed to work the motif into his art lesson every Friday. They had a shelf full of his creations. Everything from lollipop sticks to saltdough molded in to the shape of Jessica's favorite symbol.

"You won your little game," gushed his mother. "That's wonderful, darling."

"It was the county final, Mam."

"What a lovely medal! That'll give you something to remember."

Pat Shaw's gaze dropped to the floor.

Benny didn't miss it. What did she mean, remember? "What's the story, Da?"

His father put both hands on Jessica's shoulders. A united front was being presented.

"Let's wait until your brother gets here."

Benny began to get worried. They weren't a group-conference sort of family. A terrible thought occurred to him.

"Is Grandad all right?"

"What? Of course . . . No, no, Benny—Bernard—it's nothing like that."

"What's going on, then?"

"Be patient, darling. Here's Georgie now."

George traipsed into the room. He was, of course, immaculately dressed. Baggy beige corduroys and a white polo shirt.

All Benny's shirts were from the supermarket. Sometimes he found it difficult to both sneer at his brother's clothes and feel envy—at the same time. It took real effort.

"Ready, darlings?"

George smiled. Benny squinted suspiciously.

"Father has some wonderful news for you. It concerns us all, as a family."

"Lotto?"

"No, Bernard."

"You got that part in Glenroe?"

"No, Georgie, you darling. Those TV directors have not seen fit to call me, or to return my tape." Jessica sniffed delicately.

Pat Shaw took up the narrative. "You boys know we've been having some cutbacks at work."

EuroGas had been in the news recently. Some executive salary scandal. People being let go.

"You've got stamps, haven't you, Da?"

Pat smiled, nervously. "No, Benny. It's not that bad. It's good, really, a wonderful opportunity."

"What is?"

"I've been offered a promotion. Shift supervisor. It means moving."

Benny blanched. "Not Kilkenny. Tell me it's not Kilkenny. I couldn't play with the Kilkenny Cats."

"No, not Kilkenny. A bit farther afield."

Jessica had recovered from the TV snub. "It will be wonderful, darlings. A chance to study another culture."

"Oh no. It's Kerry, isn't it? Sure, they don't even know how to play hurling there!"

Jessica would have scowled, if that didn't give you wrinkles. "No, Benny . . . Bernard. This whole ordeal doesn't revolve around your proximity to a hurling pitch."

Benny didn't care about wrinkles. He scowled.

"My job will be to train the locals," continued Da. "Bring them up to speed on our procedure." He was looking at the floor again, stalling with semi-relevant information.

"Where, Da?"

Pat Shaw swallowed. "Tunisia."

The Shaw family stared into the air as though the word was flashing there. Even George was speechless. Tunisia! Where was that? What was it?

"Isn't it wonderful?" Mother's smile would have won her, at the very least, a Bafta Award for Best Actress.

Even the Crawler was fazed. "Is it?"

"Of course it is, George, darling. The company values your father's services so much that they're prepared to move the entire family to Tunisia."

"It was either that or a layoff."

"Pat! Let's give it a chance."

"Yes. Sorry. You're right . . . it seems a really good deal. Everything you could want."

"Drama club?"

"No . . . I don't think so, George."

"Hurling?"

"Well, no . . ."

"I think it's best we concentrate on the positive, everybody."

"What positive, Ma?"

Jessica winced. "Ma? Please, Bernard."

"Mam," conceded Benny.

Da got his second wind. "Sit down, the pair of you."

George and Benny, puzzled, remained seated.

"Well, shut up then!" continued Da, braving Jessica's disapproving glance. "Here's what's happening. EuroGas is in a bad way. Stocks are down. British Gas is pulling out of their slump. The domestic office can't support . . ."

Pat Shaw noticed his sons' earnest blankness.

"Aah . . . They're shutting the Wexford office down. So it's either Tunisia or the unemployment office." That was plain enough.

Benny heard the words. He understood them individually, but they didn't seem to make any sense as a sentence. Unemployment? That was for other dads. For people on the news.

"So, tell us, then!" said Benny.

"What's that?"

"This Tunisia place. Where is it?"

"Ah . . . Ah . . . North Africa."

The Crawler began to cry. Benny, alarmed, blinked back a few tears himself. Tunisia was one of those obscure little countries on the globe that he'd heard of but couldn't quite pin down. He'd been thinking maybe Eastern Europe, one of those places that used to be in Russia.

"Africa, Da?"

"North Africa. They don't have lions or elephants or anything."

"You mean we're going to Africa for the whole summer and they don't even have lions and tigers?"

Pat and Jessica Shaw glanced at each other. George was too busy blubbering to spot it. But Benny missed nothing.

"It's not just the summer, is it, Ma . . . Mam?"

"No. It's not."

George's tears dried up as though his tap had been turned off. Another benefit of speech and drama classes.

"How long, then?"

Mam took a deep breath and gave them a reassuring smile. "Your father's initial contract is for twelve months."

"A year!" Someone turned the tap back on.

"A year, Da! In some . . ."

Benny was working up to a curse. It would be his first in front of his parents. He felt the occasion merited it. But by the time he'd settled on one, his nerve was gone. Jessica rushed to comfort her distraught youngest. Da rubbed his forehead, obsessively flattening the ancestral cowlick.

2

HELL WEEK

The greatest trauma that had ever been endured by Benny Shaw was to see Wexford, his own county team, return home victorious from the Leinster Final. He couldn't decide whether he was deliriously happy or about to spontaneously explode. For weeks all thoughts of Tunisia were buried beneath a mountain of hysteria. Wexford might actually make it to the All-Ireland Final, the ultimate!

Pat Shaw, already guilty over the move, was easily manipulated into securing a pair of tickets for the semifinal. So on that historic August bank holiday weekend, father and son sat together in Croke Park. They swilled warm Fanta and chomped bashed Taytos, roaring good-natured abuse at the Offaly opposition from the safety of a purple-and-gold ocean of Wexford supporters. Both Shaws ended up hugging total strangers when the referee blew the final whistle. They even hugged each other. It was that kind of day. Wexford was in the All-Ireland

Hurling Final. It was every Wexfordman's dream. Pulling his son tight to his chest, Pat Shaw regretted the passing of this summer. His heart took a snapshot, freezing the precious moment forever. Somehow, Benny clambered up along his father's body, swinging onto his shoulders like a monkey on a branch. Pat Shaw clasped his son's ankles and added his voice to the crowd: "Up Wexford!"

But every silver lining has a cloud. The final would be scheduled for the beginning of September. They left for Tunisia in the middle of August. Maybe the young lad wouldn't be so eager to hug him then.

Family meeting. Da had picked up that phrase from *The Cosby Show* or something.

"Right, boys. Let's do a recap on our situation. We push off in two days, Saturday, the Twenty-fourth. Two flights. Dublin—Heathrow. London—Tunis. Then a jeep ride down to Sfax. Any questions?"

"I'm going to miss the final."

"That's not a question, Benny."

"It's important, though."

"I understand that, son. We're all missing it. It's a sacrifice we have to make for the family."

"Oh yeah. Georgie's real broke up over it."

Pat Shaw enunciated very clearly. "And what about me? I've been waiting for this longer than you've been alive."

"You're right," agreed Benny. "It's unfair to expect you to miss it. We should follow Mam and the Cr . . . George out."

"Benny, you're not making this easy."

"Yeah, well . . ."

"We're all making sacrifices, Bernard," added Jessica. "I'm missing the opera festival. It's the cultural event of the year."

"Oh, the pain of it."

Pat and Jessica exchanged a worried glance. Neither parent wanted to bulldoze through Benny's sarcasm. Developing psyche, and all that. Still, there was a limit to the selfishness you could put up with.

"I'm missing the most important event of my young life," continued Benny blithely. "And George, there, is missing the chance to dress up like a fairy. What a tragedy for the free world."

Pat Shaw had had enough. Only his wife's hand on his knee kept him from lunging at his son. Jessica Shaw decided that the time for niceties was past.

"Now, you listen to me, Benny," she said through a dangerous smile. Benny listened. Mam had called him Benny. Plus, her accent was slipping.

"How dare you believe your life more important than ours! How dare you put some filthy ball game before the welfare of this family! Do you think any of us want to go to some African hellhole? Well, do you?"

Benny shook his head. So did Georgie, just in case.

"Some uncivilized pit, with diseased water and mosquitoes and foreigners. What's there for me? I'll be a housewife in a prison camp. The only culture they have belonged to the Romans, for God's sake. Never trust a country where the most exciting thing that ever happened was an invasion."

Pat Shaw blinked. This was getting a bit off topic.

"But I'll go. For the family. For you! But if you don't want to—if you think your little hurley game is more important than all our well-being, then just say so and we won't go. Your father will tear up his contract and we'll try and get by on my classes. Chances are, Pat will have to go on unemployment, but as long as you see your precious match, that'll be all right. It's up to you, Benny. Think carefully before deciding the family's fate."

Eyes brimming with tears, Jessica rose and swept from the room. It was a masterful performance. She had pushed all the right buttons. She'd hit Benny with anger, guilt, and the most effective of parental tools, responsibility. Flawless. Benny was cornered. He could feel the eyes of the remaining family members on him.

"All right," he said. "I'll go."

Pat Shaw relaxed, his shoulders sinking back to their normal level. "Good man, Benny. It means a lot to me."

Benny grunted, unwilling to give up his sulk altogether.

"Now, you two go on and watch the telly. I'll see if your Mam's okay."

The brothers bolted for the remote control. Benny was closer to the door, but Georgie went through the serving hatch. They scuffled noisily, but the squealing was harmless. Pat let them off. Take your victories where you can get them. Jessica was sitting on the stairs, a handkerchief over her face.

"You are something." Pat smiled. "You nearly had me convinced."

"Nearly?" prodded Jessica.

"More than nearly," admitted Pat. "Poor old Benny, he never had a chance."

Jessica sighed. "Maybe now we can all have one."

Pat pulled her up and hugged her close.

3

THE EDGE OF THE DESERT

Grandad dropped them at the airport. Benny's two buddies actually showed up at 6 A.M. to see them off. They stood desolately by the wall, picking scabs off their elbows. Jessica felt a bit weepy at the gesture. She tousled Benny's hair.

"We can afford a minute to say good-bye to Eamonn and Niall," she whispered.

Benny dropped his O'Neills bag and trotted down to the gate. "How's it going there, lads?"

"Grand," answered Eamonn, his eyes still crusty with sleep.

"Right so," said Benny. "I'll see yez in a year."

And that was that.

"Are you sure you don't want some more time, Bernard?" asked his mother. "It's not healthy to hold back your feelings."

Benny flattened his cowlick. "I'm hardly going to kiss

them, am I? I'm ready. Are we off or what?" They loaded up the trailer without further emotional outbreak.

Benny had his hurley strapped to his chest, safely bound in sports socks. He caused a few minor glitches at the airport, setting off the metal detector because of the metal band on the hurley, and generally giving the impression of being a threat to civilized living. But they finally boarded. Georgie was sad wishing his grandad farewell, Benny distraught over losing a steady source of fivers.

Heathrow Airport was as busy and rushed as Dublin, but at last they boarded TUNISAIR flight TU-790 and were soon flying over France at eight hundred miles per hour. Benny lounged in his seat—this flying thing was old hat to him already, on the second flight of his life. He was trying not to stare at the other passengers. A lot of them were foreigners. Tunisians. Most of them didn't look African, not like you'd expect. Not like in *Zulu* or the Tarzan films. More Arab or Italian. Plus, they all seemed to be from one family. Roaring at one another down the length of the plane. A gregarious, smiley bunch.

The plane nosed into its descent. The pilot proved to be a bit of a free spirit. By the time the tires scraped tarmac, he'd performed every possible aerial maneuver with the exception of a victory roll. They bounced along, one wheel at a time, slowing to a shuddering halt.

The Tunisian passengers erupted in spontaneous applause, lighting up celebratory cigarettes. With much hugging and slapping of shoulders, they clambered up on the seats, emptying out the overhead lockers. It was incredible that so much could be crammed into such small spaces. There were quilts and bicycles. Chairs and lamps. Satellite dishes and baby strollers. Benny could have sworn that one sack wriggled as it passed him. He decided to ignore it.

The Shaws smelled Tunisia before they saw it. When the doors were finally cracked open, the outside air flooded in. It was heavy and sweet, with hints of spices and sweat. It made you sleepy and excited, as though the culture of the country was woven through its oxygen. The Tunisians were climbing over one another to get out the door, but the Shaws were frozen, nervous, now that the enormity of their move was upon them.

Da broke the spell. "Right, you crowd," he said, reaching for the bags. "Let's get a move on. There should be a car waiting."

Two hours later, with the last evening rays of the sun bouncing off the one-way security glass, the car was still waiting. The Shaws' luggage somehow hadn't made the connection and was stranded in Heathrow. Benny stared at the baggage conveyer, convinced that if he looked hard enough his gear bag would come lurching through the flaps. What he was really doing was ignoring his surroundings. It was all too much. The heat sapped his natural doggedness and wrapped around him like an electric blanket. His layers of clothing hung off him in soppy ropes.

Pat Shaw was embroiled in a frustrating discussion with a customs man and the EuroGas driver. One spoke mostly French, the other only Arabic, and Da had just English in a Wexford accent. It was a linguist's nightmare.

"No bags," said Pat. "Bags gone."

"Pas de baggage," explained the driver to the customs man.

"Yes!" enthused Da. A breakthrough. "Paddy's baggage. That's it."

Benny looked around at the people. They weren't Irish, for a start. Now Benny was no eejit, he wasn't expecting the Tunisian nationals to be Irish. What he did expect was darkish people with Irishy personalities. That was not what he got. The Tunisians weren't interested in conforming to Benny's preconceptions. They stubbornly insisted on being themselves. You couldn't even categorize them. Successive waves of Muslim and European invaders, combined with darker genes from south of the Sahara, made appearances unpredictable. It was like every race in the world was focused here. One second you were looking at a black lad all dressed up like one of them rappers, the next some little red-haired, pale-faced chap was trying to sell you flowers.

Da eventually gave up wrangling with the customs guy. He rejoined his family, talking to the ground. He was mad. Fuming. Benny had seen him like this only on one previous occasion: a little mix-up over report cards and forged signatures. Mam linked his arm, and it cooled him down, as it always did.

"The situation is this," said Da, his voice raised over the surrounding hubbub. "We're going to head off to Sfax, and they'll send the bags down when they get here."

"If," interjected Benny.

Da glared at him. "Don't start on me, Benny. I'm still not over all those delays in customs. You and that hurley! I feel like breaking it across your behind."

The one thing about Da was that he never bluffed. Benny hugged his hurley protectively. They were in Africa now. The threat of having your children removed by social services was no longer valid. It was even conceivable that they could sell him to slave traders!

The family straggled out to the jeep. As they outdistanced the last breath of whatever air conditioning there was, the temperature and humidity soared in a matter of inches. Benny felt a wall of heat suck the breath from his lungs.

The jeep, at least, was not a disappointment. Strictly

speaking, it wasn't actually a Jeep jeep, it was a Land Rover Discovery. The driver let them in, unlocking the doors with a remote. Fairly knacky, all right, thought Benny, duly impressed. He clambered into the back, the vehicle's height separating him from his surroundings. He could almost pretend he was in the back of a bus at home. He closed his eyes and hunkered down low, but it was no use. Africa wouldn't go away.

The city flashed by their speeding vehicle. They hared along at an inordinate pace. And everywhere the Tunisians argued as they went. They hung out the windows hollering, tooted their horns incessantly, and piled whole families on fragile mopeds.

Benny realized he was nodding off, a haze was settling over his vision. His drooping senses picked out details from the roadside. Kids selling flowers at the traffic lights, risking mortal injury under the wheels of Libyan tankers. They should be in bed, not cracking their toenails on rough tarmac. Benny fought sleep, holding one eye open. There was much more to see. Georgie had passed out. But he, the mighty Bernard, would outlast the Crawler. This was Africa. Wonders lurked around every corner. Don't miss it. Don't . . .

Benny was in Africa, asleep, thousands of miles from home. His brain had gone into overload and decided to shut down. The two brothers snuggled close, snoring and drooling all over each other. You could almost feel the tension seeping out of the jeep.

Benny was awake again. Happened every morning. But something had woken him. Something besides the strangeness. It sounded as though a van was turning over outside his door. He sat up. He was in a small rectangular room. Benny wasn't known for being much of a style guru, but compared to the chaps who did this room, he could be writing for *Cosmo*-whatever. There was a horrendous quilt draped over the bed that for some reason reminded him of a stomach bug he'd once had. The curtains were pink. You're probably thinking, how lovely, pastel pink. Wrong. This was shiny, reflective pink. Watery, cream emulsion covered the walls so that the plasterboard showed through. There were two units in the room: a desk with wickerwork drawers and a mismatched deep brown, fake teak wardrobe. Benny immediately loved it. Now here was a room you wouldn't be afraid to wreck. If he kicked a few balls into the beige skirting board, Ma would probably thank him.

So this was Sfax. Chilly enough all the same. Right old breeze coming in through that vent. Benny's throat was dried up by the cold air. Then he remembered air conditioning. That was it. Must have an engine big enough to power a tractor.

The same maniac decorator had been let loose in the sitting room. Same lurid curtains and bland gray carpet. The stomach-bug pattern had been carried over to the three-piece suite. A few squat multipurpose units were dotted along the walls. Benny threw himself onto the couch. It defied him, keeping its shape. He beat it with elbows and knees. Soon, he thought, you will be mine.

Benny didn't study the kitchen much. It was grand, he supposed. There was a heap of kitcheny stuff. Cookers and that. Nothing much in the fridge. A couple of cartons of orange juice. Benny tore one open and squirted half its contents down his throat. He had no idea what time it was. Early. There wasn't a peep from the other rooms. Probably worn out after the journey. His hurley was propped in a corner. Benny grabbed it and dug a tennis ball from his O'Neills bag. He wasn't going to risk the precious sliotar in an unknown environment.

When he opened the front door, Benny realized just how effective the AC was. Humidity flowed in like hot honey, along with yesterday's smells. The sun throbbed on his scalp. The Irish boy hopped outside into the nearest shadow. Of course the dreaded cowlick was now at full mast.

He took a good look around Marhaba village—apparently Marhaba meant "welcome," or something. "Village" was a bit of an optimistic name for this place. "Camp," he decided, was a bit more honest. The identical boxlike units curved down to the gate. They looked like portacabins. The roofs were flat—obviously no one was expecting rain. Benny hopped down the narrow garden, trying to stay out of the sun. The grass bounced under his feet. Benny stopped to examine it. Playing surfaces were very important to him. You couldn't really call it grass. More like scutch, or springy weed. The sandy clay was visible through the sparse growth. You'd give yourself some skinning taking a tumble on that stuff. It'd be good for sidelines, though. A sliotar could balance up on one blade.

Benny ambled down toward the gate. A big barred barricade. It looked like they were trying to keep out more than dogs. There were even spotlights and a guardhouse. Fairly paranoid sort of setup for a stable country. There was a chap standing by the gate. A big Tunisian fellow in a blue jumpsuit. He had Docs on him, laced all the way up his shins. His bald head would blind you, if the sun caught him at the right angle.

Benny gave him a nod, but your man was having none of the friendliness bit. He's probably scared, thought Benny. His orders are not to get overfamiliar with the white man. He flashed the man his sincerest smile.

"Howza goin' there?"

The man glared at him through slitted eyes. Other children might have been scared by the guard's snarling visage, but Benny Shaw had yet to meet an adult that could catch him.

"Howza goin?" repeated Benny gamely.

"English only," grunted the guard.

"Huh?"

"English. I speak just English."

"Yeah. I'm just after asking you how's the form?"

The man enunciated carefully. "Een-gel-ish only."

Benny retreated, never suspecting that his strong Wexford accent could be the culprit. He gave the guard a scowl and journeyed on.

The village was enclosed by a high wall. Not that high, though. Benny thought he could manage it with a good run. The whole area was dead flat, with strange, ancient-looking trees dotted between the houses. It was as though someone had planted a roomful of arthritic pensioners. These were the famous olive trees, he supposed. Benny followed the blacktop road around, stepping over huge speed bumps. The camp seemed to be roughly circular in shape, with two rows of living units in one half, and an assortment of buildings in the other. But right there in the center, surrounded by a low wall of red ornamental brickwork, was the pool. An outdoor swimming pool! Benny's pulse quickened. At last, a plus to this whole African thing.

As he neared the pool, gurgling, laughing noises mingled with the splashing. Sounded like girls. Mixed feelings on that score. He didn't despise them with the same passion that he used to. In fact, Benny suspected that there would come a time in the not-too-distant future when he might develop a mysterious interest in them. There was a railed-off baby pool before the main job. A couple of young lads were splashing around in a half foot of water. Their mother, or whatever, was lounging on a chaise in the shade. The boys gave Benny that wide-eyed, tongues-out look reserved for strangers. Benny responded with a snarl and a shake of the hurley. You had to sort the nippers out early or they might get cheeky.

There was a sandpit with a couple of animal slides in it. Benny crawled up an elephant's back. He still couldn't see much of the main pool area. It sounded excellent, though. Music, roaring, and laughter. He felt a twinge of hope. Benny slid down the trunk and tapped the tennis ball off ahead of him. It rolled "accidentally" to the pool wall. Sure, then of course, Benny had to go get it. With an exasperated expression his ma would be proud of, he trotted over to the wall. Rubbing the dust from his tennis ball, Benny nonchalantly peeked through the cavities. What he saw there made him forget he wasn't looking.

There was a gang of them horsing around in the pool. This in itself was not a particularly startling event. It wasn't as though Benny had never seen a swimming pool before. Half the school went across the bridge to

Ferrybank pool every Wednesday. The Saint Jerome's excursions involved dive-bombing, frantic dog-paddling in the shallow end, and more than a few chancers trying to pass off boxer shorts as swimming trunks.

These kids in front of him looked like they were out of a Budget Travel ad. Most of them were bleached blond by the sun. Their hair looked grand, even after a soaking. When Benny emerged from any wet environment you'd swear someone had dropped a wet rat on his head. Their togs were expensive-looking too. Benny thought of his own multipurpose clothes. He was starting to feel decidedly uncultured. A tall girl launched herself from the diving board. She was pretty and tanned. Long brown legs slicing the water. Benny glanced at his own knees. Whatever wasn't scabbed and flaky was an anemic blue-white.

Benny decided he wasn't ready for this yet. He'd just take a few days to let the bruises on his legs heal up. Maybe plaster some of Ma's mousse on the cowlick. His reticence shocked him. Usually he'd be in like a shot, plowing up and down the pool with the best of them. He was well able to swim. But these guys had loads of fancy little flicks and kicks that would make him look like a plodder. That would be mortifying altogether. Time to move on.

Benny noticed the floodlights before he saw the field. Big ones, too. There weren't a dozen pitches in the whole of

Ireland with lights like that. There were eight towering structures for holding the lights, four on the full-sized pitch and four more wasted on tennis courts. Of course, the goals were squat rectangles. Soccer only. You couldn't practice properly on them. Benny had been hoping for rugby posts, at least, with uprights like hurling posts. You could lose all sorts of accuracy in a couple of weeks, never mind a year. There were portable sprinklers all over the place. Benny stroked the grass. Whatever they were pumping in was working. It was like a carpet. You wouldn't get a better surface in Croke Park. The back of Benny's neck was beginning to tingle—he'd better get out of this sun pretty sharpish. Maybe just a couple of pulls with the hurley to loosen up the arm.

He lobbed the ball to shoulder height and pulled his hurley across it, loading it with topspin. In his mind, the ball was speeding toward the top corner of the net. In the real world, however, it was pulling high and right. Tennis balls! Stupid thing was probably expanding in the heat or something. Benny watched in utter disgust as the ball bounced off into the scrub. He trotted in pursuit, but stopped after a dozen paces. This heat was too ferocious. Should've been nicer to those kids in the baby pool, he thought ruefully, might be glad for a gofer later.

The ball was nestled in the depths of a bristly bush. Benny whacked it out, dislodging a dozen monstrous ants in the process. Maybe he'd have a go at a few shots off the ground. Nothing too strenuous. He set himself up near the goal. Your tennis balls were grand for sitting up on the grass, but as soon as the air got under them they'd nearly go into orbit. He sliced up a big sod of turf, and the ball spun erratically away to the left. Benny chased after it, fuming. Another bandy shot! Of course it was all the ball's fault. Had to be. He took a vengeful running swing at it. Total miss this time. Another divot of clay exploded around his shins.

A huge roar from the sidelines stopped his wild pucking. Your man, the guard, was haring across the field toward him, bellowing like a branded bull. Benny took a half step backward, then stopped. If the baldy fellow kept on at that pace, his best bet was a neat side step.

The guard halted before Benny, showing surprising deceleration for a big hulk.

"Howye," said Benny genially.

The guard wiped a sheen of sweat from his brow. He picked up the dislodged clay.

"Earth!" he said.

Benny nodded. "Uh-huh." There was earth in Ireland.

"You break the earth," grunted the guard, trying to swallow some inexplicable anger. Benny plucked the mucky blob from his huge hands and stamped it into the ground.

"I fix the earth," he grinned. This was the height of cheek, but it felt good.

"This field is not for sticks to beat."

"Fairly good English there!"

"Pardon?"

"What?"

The guard was a big man. Having to reason with boys did not sit well with him.

"Workers make this field," he said in a throaty voice. "It takes two years to make Europeans happy. Now you beat it with your stick."

Benny balked. "This is not a stick. This is a precision instrument."

The unfortunate combination of the syrupy Wexford accent and Benny brandishing his instrument caused the guard to react. He made a lunge for the hurley. Quick hands, too. He got a hold on it before Benny could move it. Instinct took over. Benny could almost hear Father Barty roaring from the sideline as he twisted, reversed his shoulders, and backed into his attacker. As soon as he heard the air puff from the guard's chest, he set off running. Those little reverse fouls were lovely. Do it at the right angle and the ref would swear the other lad was at fault.

Benny debated whether or not to retrieve the tennis ball. He decided against it. Your man could have a machete or some curare-tipped darts down the inside of his jumpsuit. Maybe butchering an Irish boy wasn't even a crime in this part of the world. Probably a misdemeanor. The guard would get off with a light scolding and no telly for a week.

Da was listening to someone on the other end of the line, but he was glaring at his elder son. Benny made a game attempt to maintain an innocent face, but Ma and Georgie were giving him the eye from the stomach-bug couch.

"Yes . . . ah, *oui*," said Da. "Yes, I realize that. I know that. Yes, I'll tell the boy." It was obvious that all this obsequiousness was gagging Da on the way up.

"He knows he's not at home anymore. Yes, I'm sure. Thank you again, Mr. Gama . . ." Pat Shaw's gaze softened for an instant. "Oh, and one more thing, if you ever lay a finger on my boy again you better have your VHI paid up . . . What? It's medical insurance."

Da slammed the receiver down, his one-liner gone disastrously awry. Benny suspected he'd be blamed for that too. "Well?"

"Well, what?"

"Don't start, Benny."

"There's a pitch up there, so I had a few pucks."

"Your man Gama made it sound like you were plowing that field."

"Hardly!"

"Plus, you gave him a dig in the ribs."

Benny shrugged. "He tackled me."

Pat Shaw sat beside his wife. There were advantages and disadvantages to being a nineties parent. On the positive side, your children only had themselves to blame if they grew up maladjusted. The negative aspect was that you had to spend a large chunk of your life trying to argue logically with a person who had never admitted to being wrong in his short life. Sometimes Pat hankered for the days when children with points of view were considered impudent, and instantly chastised.

"This is not your ordinary field," he explained. "Everything is imported. Topsoil, seed, fertilizer, the whole shebang. Took them about two years to get it soccer-worthy. Even the Tunisian national team doesn't have a pitch like this."

"I just got here, you know. No one told me any of this."

Da was on a roll now. "They had twenty men crawling down the length of that field on hands and knees, picking out the weeds."

"Right. I get the message."

"It's an investment of sweat and labor."

"Ah here, Da. Let's not get carried away."

George shook with anticipation. Benny never knew when he was going too far.

"Just keep it up now, boyo, and you'll be grounded," Da warned.

Benny was not one to pass up a chance for sarcasm. "Oh no! Please don't ground me. Please, Papa, don't stop me from being fried and mugged."

Georgie nearly vibrated off the sofa. Jessica dug her nails into her husband's leg, but Pat Shaw was about to have a flashback to fifties-style parenting.

There was a knock at the door. Luck of the Irish. Da changed direction in mid-lunge, trying to transform his grimace to a welcoming smile. He didn't quite manage it.

"What?" he snarled at their first visitor. The man took an anxious step backward, sheltering behind a officious clipboard.

"Ah . . . Mr. Shaw?"

Da nodded, not trusting himself to civility. The man extended a hand.

"Talal Khayssi. Village manager. We have a three o'clock induction."

"Yes, Mr. Khayssi. Come in, please."

The diminutive Tunisian stepped warily over the threshold. Europeans were unstable. You had to treat them like large dogs: easy to train but unreliable in a crisis. His eyes were huge behind thick glasses and his high forehead was lined with drops of sweat.

"Fierce hot today," commented Pat, trying out his voice.

"*Oui* . . . Yes. The heat is . . . fierce."

Benny thought that perhaps it was fairly scaldy here most days, and maybe the Africans didn't chat as much about the weather as the Irish.

"Sit down, please." Da's social style clicked in. Khayssi took a seat. "This is Jessica, my wife, and my boys, George and Bernard."

Khayssi stood again and did a formal round of handshaking.

Mam took over. "Would you like something to drink, Mr. Khayssi?"

It seemed like he would. His white shirt was pasted to his belly and his tie looked like a snaky water balloon.

"Yes, please. That would be pleasant."

They sat smiling like eejits until Mam returned. Khayssi took a dainty sip, placing the glass on the coffee table.

"Shall we begin?"

Nods.

"Very well." He cleared his throat for a spiel. "Here in Africa, things are not the same as in Europe."

"You don't say," muttered Benny, feeling cheated out of a sulk.

"There are certain things to be wary of."

"Big baldy guards."

"Bernard!"

"Sorry Ma . . . Mam."

"If, for example, you are stung by a scorpion—"

"Pardon me?"

"A scorpion, Madam. A small insectoid with a poisonous sting. Indigenous to Africa."

"I know what a scorpion is, Mr. Khayssi."

"Do not worry, Madam. In three years we have only seen one scorpion in Marhaba village. And never once a snake."

Benny stopped pouting and started paying attention. "Snakes? Now, hold on there!"

Talal Khayssi smiled indulgently. "Please, young man, let me continue. If, and this is a big if, you are stung by a scorpion, you have more than one hour to get to a hospital."

"Oh sure, that's grand, then."

"Benny! Sarcasm in not going to help us here."

"There is a nurse at the plant. And I have here a paper which says, 'I have been bitten by a scorpion' in French and Arabic."

"What about English?"

"I presumed that you spoke English, Mr. Shaw. In any event, the nurse's English is not so good."

"That's reassuring."

"Do not waste energy fretting over this, Mrs. Shaw. The chances of this happening are minuscule."

Benny and Da were both absently slapping their cowlicks.

"What about snakes then?" asked Da.

Talal Khayssi stared at his clipboard. "Snakes, as I say, have never been seen in the village. They do not like to climb walls." He laughed. Nervous laughter. "Also, your children are too big to be eaten whole."

George paled. Benny knew he should smirk on principle, but his stomach felt like a spin dryer at the moment.

"There is a possibility that a small reptile may slither beneath the gate bars, under the cover of night. If any of the family are bitten, please note the color of the snake and proceed to the plant immediately."

"Any particular color we should worry about?"

"No, no, Mr. Shaw. Most venoms only cause nausea and swelling . . . except maybe black. Worry about black. But, as I say, no snakes have been seen in the village. They are very rare north of the Sahara. It has been a long time, months in fact, since we have had a fatality in Sfax."

Jessica grabbed Khayssi's water and drank it in several gulps.

"And then there's HIV," continued the village manager brightly.

"Oh Jesus, Mary, and Joseph," breathed Jessica.

"Actually, there's far less chance of contracting that particular virus here than in the UK. But just to be on the safe side, always ask for a fresh razor at the barber's."

"Fresh razor, righto."

"Quiet, Bernard!" snapped Da. "Do you have any good news, Khayssi?" No more "Mr."

"Of course." Talal Khayssi beamed. "Your vehicle has arrived. It is a Toyota Landcruiser, four-wheel drive."

Da fought against grinning, but lost. Placing your children in mortal danger wasn't quite so bad when you had a big shiny jeep parked in the driveway.

"There is a hand-held radio on the dash. Charge it every night and keep it with you on all road journeys. You are . . . ah . . . Zulu Three. Central is Bravo One."

"In case of breakdowns, is it?"

"Yes, and accidents. Locals get a bit upset if one of our own is injured. It's usually our own fault. The youths are very erratic on mopeds. Be especially careful during Ramadan. Drivers are often fasting and light-headed. If there is an accident, lock your doors and drive straight to the station of the Garde Nationale."

"Or?"

"Or if there is a fundamentalist onlooker, he may attempt to incite a riot."

"A riot! We were told this was a stable country!"

"It is, Madam," protested Khayssi. "I am presenting worst-case scenarios. These things are possible but highly unlikely."

"I see."

The Tunisian noticed his glass was empty. He stood to leave.

"Oh, and one more item. Please take extra care when crossing the railway tracks. The warning lights are often not operational. We have lost one vehicle already this year."

"Aah . . ." croaked Da, the shine on his jeep fading by the second.

"I'll just leave you these requisition forms," added Khayssi. "If you need anything, call me at the office."

After another round of handshakes, Talal Khayssi let himself out. The Shaws sat in silence for a while, then Mam decided she needed to have a talk with her husband. In private. Benny suddenly felt the weight of Africa bearing down on him. He pulled himself out of the armchair and went for a nap.

What he didn't know was that it wouldn't be a scorpion or a snake that got him that afternoon. Instead, a tiny little mosquito droned into his room, anesthetized Benny's forehead, and sucked a few drops of blood out of him. This was a pity, since Benny was allergic to mosquitoes.

4

EDUCATIONAL ENVIRONMENT

Benny couldn't believe it. He'd known, in theory, there was life before eight thirty, but never had any desire to actually experience it. It was now only seven thirty, and he and the Crawler were slouched on the sofa, dribbling cornflakes down their chins. Ma was shuffling around in zombie mode, stuffing lunch into Tupperware containers. Benny felt another glob of mashed cereal slide down his throat. These were cornflakes in name only. Your Kellogg's variety would stay crisp for minutes, but these imposters turned soggy after a mere lick of the milk.

Jessica Shaw dropped a lunch box on the table and aimed a few air kisses at the boys' heads.

"Once more into the bed, dear friends," she droned, sleepwalking off down the corridor.

George was looking a bit tearful.

"Why don't you have a sob?" suggested Benny. "Seeing as you're only a big baby anyway."

George said nothing, but he didn't cry either. He swallowed a mouthful of cereal and stomped off to brush his teeth. Benny sighed; even harassing the Crawler wasn't hitting the mark this morning.

It was ten to eight, and they couldn't put it off any longer. Benny was seething at the unfairness of if all. The boys in Wexford still had fourteen long days of holidays and hurling ahead of them, with the All-Ireland Final to round it off. And here he was, trekking off to a new school at some ungodly hour in the morning with an itchy red lump smack in the middle of his forehead.

The heat wasn't too ferocious yet. Typical schoolyard rumblings echoed through the dead air. The brothers stopped close to the fence. There were kids all over a huge jungle gym. They swung, climbed, and slid, their mouths big circles of joy. Benny hung back, trying to spot the gang leader. Surely there'd be some big greasy bullyboy on hand to sort out the new lads.

It was futile. He couldn't even see the gang. The whole place had a clean feeling about it. Too good to be true. He'd be willing to bet none of these guys had ever picked up head lice in a scuffle.

George pushed through the swing gate. It swished back, cracking his older brother on the shin. Benny whistled nonchalantly through the pain. He grabbed the handle of Georgie's backpack, thinking that perhaps a little rabbit punch to the kidneys would be suitable retribution, but the girl from the pool was watching him. Blue eyes sparkled beneath blond bangs. Benny felt a gommy smile spread unbidden across his face. Then his native Irish cynicism hacked through the mist like an ice pick—she was only being friendly from a distance. Wait till she saw him close up: bandy legs, scabby knees, and a red lump between his eyes. Benny felt a defensive scowl settle over his features.

Benny's thoughts were disturbed by the ringing of a small bell. A middle-aged couple was standing on the school steps. The woman was dinging one of those little triangles. Interesting. Presumably everyone would ignore this sad effort. But no. The students all scampered into two short lines, grinning at the prospect of going in to work. Benny shuddered. Maniacs.

Even with the whole school assembled, there wasn't enough for one Irish class. Benny counted twelve in all. All fairly clean, too. No greasy heads or hand-me-down jumpers. The woman spoke. "Morning, kids."

American. Speaking through her nose like that one in *Hello Dolly*.

"We've got two new little guys this morning. All the way from the Emerald Isle, begorrah."

"Top of the mornin'," enthused George in his best Leprechaun.

Benny tried to disguise his grimace as a grin.

The woman smiled at the cute Irish guys. She was around the sixty mark, with a heap of necklaces hanging on her chest. All natural stuff. Bits of tree and glazed berries. Her face had the walnutty, wrinkled look of a life-long outdoorsy type. Hippie, decided Benny. His ma had a few of those in her women's group back home. Her partner was Italian looking, with a head of wild gray hair and a huge German pipe hanging out of his gob. My parents are entrusting me to a pair of love children, thought Benny ruefully.

"First, we should introduce ourselves," continued the woman. "I am Principal Rossi, and this is my husband, Roberto."

"Good morning, Principal Rossi, Mr. Rossi," said George.

"Howye," said Benny.

"We don't stand on ceremony here." Roberto Rossi smiled. "Don't think of us as fuddy-duddy grown-ups. We're your buddies. When someone calls out 'Hey, Mr. Rossi,' I look around for my dad."

The whole school chuckled fondly.

"So please, guys, call us Harmony and Bob," gushed Harmony.

Harmony and Bob? Oh, George was going to love this school. He'd been out of place all of his life, but finally he was home. At St. Jerome's, calling a teacher by his Christian name was only slightly less serious than classroom arson. There were skin-headed, tattooed, pit bull owners in Wexford who still trembled at the sight of a Christian Brothers uniform.

"George and Bernard Shaw," noted Bob Rossi from their enrollment slips. "I like it. You two got some right-on parents."

"Yeah, we're lucky guys," grinned George, getting more cosmopolitan by the second.

Oh please, thought Benny. Only two minutes, and the Crawler was already doing the accent.

"Now, you kids. How can we show these two Irish boys that we feel for them?"

A little sprog piped up: "Group hug!"

"Good idea: love-huddle. Remember, positive emotions only."

The students surrounded Benny and George, arms out like brainthirsty zombies. Benny fought his natural instinct to run. He was a forward. And a forward's job is to beat your way through anyone within a meter's radius. The human circle gushed forward, and the Shaw brothers were hugged at all levels. It was like being in the middle of a huddle. Naturally, Georgie loved it. He'd been at this sort of thing for years in drama class. George was in touch with his feminine side, and all that. Benny wouldn't even admit to having a feminine side, never mind touch it.

An eternity later they backed off, leaving Benny with the imprints of a hundred fingers crawling over his body. Harmony tinkled the triangle again.

"Okay, guys, maybe you could answer a question that's been bugging me. There are two words I don't understand. Do you know what they are?"

"*Can't* and *won't*," came the reply.

"Right! And you have my permission not to learn those words. They're just *can* and *will* plus negative attitude."

All this cutesy stuff was making Benny's flesh crawl. Surely nobody actually believed any of it? Surely it could never get results?

They all bounced inside, chatting and smiling. George was an instant celebrity. His hair seemed to have realigned itself to the preppy style of the other nine-year-olds. Benny, on the other hand, felt a chasm of differences yawning between him and the rest of them. He picked the line with the tallest kids and shuffled to the back of it.

Benny immediately embarked on the age-old process of seeing how far he could push the teacher. It was written in the Bible somewhere that you had to sort out, or be sorted, on your first day.

"Okay, you guys," said the principal. "Let's get rolling with some language arts."

"Eh . . . Miss?"

"Harmony."

"Sorry, Harmony?"

"Yes, Benny?"

"What language would that be?"

Harmony came over and ruffled his hair. "English, of course."

"It's just that English is the language of the oppressor and all that."

"That's okay, honey. We'll just put in a few *howdy*s and *y'all*s and call it American."

Not bad, thought Benny grudgingly. Time for a tactical retreat.

"Can I go to the jacks?"

Harmony's smile widened. "You probably mean bathroom. 'Jacks,' that's a scream. Stateside we say 'the john.' I prefer that cute little English word, 'loo.' We don't want to embarrass the other guys."

Benny looked around. The other guys did look a bit sheepish.

"Go right ahead, Benny. Don't take all day, though, or I'll have to send in the SWAT team."

That wasn't bad, either. The woman had a sense of humor.

He sat on the loo, ruminating. This Rossi woman was using affection to nail him. Benny had heard of this tactic before; he'd just never personally witnessed it. He'd have to perpetrate something really vile to make her lose her temper. Benny wasn't sure why he had to go through this ritual. It was tradition. Respect had to be earned by both sides.

Benny stomped back up the stairs, bursting in the door with as much violence as possible. No one even looked up. They were busy hammering into some books. This wasn't natural. Your average student was only too delighted to be distracted. Mrs. Rossi was moving among her charges, ruffling hair, smiling fondly. It was that affection thing again. This Harmony woman seemed to actually care about these eejits. Benny smiled nastily. Suddenly it become obvious how he could bring this hippie to the boiling point. He'd use her own compassion against her. This may seem like a cruel tactic, but our hero was not used to the idea of coming to school to learn. Not voluntarily, at any rate. In his experience, it was the teacher's job to coerce him into learning reams of useless information—such as quadratic equations. It was his duty, as a student, to avoid with every breath in his body ingesting these worthless facts.

"Now, Bernard."

"Benny."

"Benny. I think you've had time to get your bearings, so maybe you'd like to join in with the class?"

"Okeydokey."

"Good boy. So perhaps you can tell us the capital of Chile?"

Benny frowned in concentration. "Eh . . . that'd be C, Miss."

"Excuse me?"

"C," repeated Benny. "Chile'd be a proper noun, so C would be the capital."

Harmony's face was a mask of kindness, but she was reeling mentally. Could the Irish guy possibly be that stupid? She'd heard stories, of course, but that was just bad press.

"No, Benny, I meant capital city."

"Oh," said Benny, letting his tongue loll out slightly.

The blond girl came to his rescue.

"It's Santiago, Harmony." Nice wee Scottish accent.

"Thank you, Grace."

Later they were doing a crossword.

"Okay . . . An American Indian might hurl this at his enemies. Eight letters, first four: T . . . O . . . M . . . A . . . Benny?"

Benny chewed his lip. "Ah . . . It wouldn't be tomatoes, would it?"

Harmony was beginning to suspect something. Benny could see the hot-blooded European heritage rising. Victory on the horizon.

Harmony made a time-out sign with her hands. Wordlessly, everybody rose and proceeded to a circle of cushions at the rear of the room. They sat facing one another. Weirder and weirder. "Come on, Benny. It's time we had a little talk."

Harmony patted a Snoopy cushion beside her. Benny moped over and sat down. Somehow this circle of friendly faces terrified him more than the hairiest back he'd ever played against.

"Okay, guys, you all know the rules. Say whatever you want, so long as it's positive, and nothing leaves the circle. Anybody?"

"Benny's having problems adjusting," said Grace.

"Good."

"He's not accustomed to our educational-orientated environment," added the Oriental guy.

"Excellent, James."

"Yeah, thanks, James."

"Now, now, Benny. Sarcasm is an absolute no-no."

"Well, excuse me."

"Bernard!"

"Sorry."

It was a clever trick, whatever was going on. After eight years' experience, Benny usually had the teacher's angle figured in seconds. There were only a few basic approaches. The "You should be ashamed of yourself" spiel, the "You're on your last chance" effort, and the "I wouldn't bother if you were stupid" speech. This could be any of those, or a combination of all three.

"Now, Benny. If we're gonna assimilate you into our happy group, we'll have to deal with this dumb attitude you're faking."

Benny was stunned. All he could do was gape at this elfin woman bent over by the weight of her necklaces. This was not the way the game was played. The teacher never acknowledged that there was a problem, much less baldly stated what it was. "I don't know what you're talking about," he spluttered. "I am dopey. Honest!"

Harmony smiled kindly. "Comments?"

James raised a professorial finger. "I think that Benny is intimidated."

"By?"

"New surroundings."

"So, how can we help?"

A tall girl with a spiky blond crop waved her hand.

"Zoe?"

Zoe, thought Benny. Oh my God.

"We should, like, talk about ourselves, you know, make ourselves, like, familiar."

Another Yank. From one of those cool cities, with beaches and skateboards.

"Maybe Benny could ask us some questions too."

"Good idea, Ed."

Ed was English.

"That should help to demystify our situation. Nullify some of those nasty insecurities that Benny's feeling. Okay, Heather, why don't you start?"

Heather smiled through tombstone braces. Benny saw now that she must be Ed's sister.

"Hi, Benny. I'm Heather. Me and Ed, sorry, Ed and I are from Liverpool. That's in England."

"Is it?"

"Benny!"

"Sorry."

"Da's here on a three-year contract. We live in a villa in town with its own pool. That's because there are three children in our family. Baby John is still a baby."

"Grace?"

"I'm from Edinburgh. I won't say where that is or you'll probably be smart."

Benny felt like a worm.

"I don't have any brothers or sisters. I'm your next-door neighbor. Oh, I've been here for fourteen months now. My hobbies are swimming and football."

Benny nodded and gave his best genuine smile.

"Me next," said Zoe.

Harmony nodded.

"Oh . . . Ah . . . gosh, well. I'm Zoe. Cool name,

huh? Well, actually it's Alicia, but that's so, like, every-where these days. So I changed it by personal vow. I've got, like, two brothers but they're in college state-side. My dad's the site manager. His wife does some beauty work from her chalet and my mom is back in San Diego."

It took Benny a minute to figure that one out.

"I adore, like, all the English pop groups, fake tattoos, piercing, and *Melrose Place*, which is not available in this backward country . . ."

Harmony frowned.

". . . although I totally respect this developing African culture and appreciate the opportunity I've been given to live here."

That sounded a bit rotelike.

"Your turn, Bernard."

Benny took a breath. "Benny Shaw. Twelve. Irish. One brother. Hurling."

"Okay. Maybe you have a few queries for your new classmates?"

"Don't think so."

"I gotta question for you, Benny. How come you're acting so ornery? That's Texan for awkward."

Benny squinted at the attentive faces. Feed them a harmless truth. Something that Harmony's psychology diploma was just dying to hear.

"It's the . . . ah," he struggled to remember the phrase, "trauma of relocation."

Harmony put an arm around him. "That problem's an old thorn for every kid here. You leave your friends, your school. It's like being ripped from the womb."

Benny winced. He hadn't thought of it like that.

"You're hurtin', Benny. Don't keep it inside."

She was right. He was hurtin'!

"This place. Well, it's all so different. At St. Jerome's, my old school, we had fighting and lads smoking and Christian Brothers who'd tan your hide as quick as look at you."

The pupils' eyes widened. Oh, the horror!

Benny had them. He decided to go for broke. "We'd no pool, or basketball courts. You'd never dream of calling the teachers by their first names. The principal used to give sly beatings up the ball alley. There'd be vicious matches against the other schools and the secondary lads would have cider parties on the weekends. . . ."

Benny paused. Even Harmony was dumbstruck.

Benny sniffed noisily. "I miss all that stuff!"

After school Benny decided to go for a puck-about. For a bit of sanity. Gama was guarding the pitch. The sinking sun gave his bald head a shiny skull cap.

"Go on, ye big baldy eejit," said Benny in the tone of a

greeting. The guard made some complicated hand gestures. Odds on it wasn't a blessing. With the pitch staked out, he'd have to find some other open space for a few smacks of the ball.

They were obviously having a right laugh up beside the pool. Georgie's kicked-piglet laugh shattered the air. He'd have the cutesy bit cranked up to the limit.

Feeling heroically excluded, Benny sulked off to find the Marhaba village's equivalent of a black hole. He knew he was there when Gama stopped following him. Obviously no one cared what he did to this hellhole. The area was littered with construction debris: red cavity blocks, concrete lakes, and twisted steel rods springing from the ground like robotic trees. Real death-trap stuff. The builders had bleached every bit of vegetation out of the ground, so he might even be able to avoid getting bitten. But best of all, it was wedged in behind the squash courts, so he couldn't be seen from the path.

There was an old barrel on its end up by the wall. Target practice. Benny tossed his spare tennis ball to eye level and pulled his hurley up over it. The ball whirred in a downward arc, juddering into the back of the barrel. Rust flakes took flight like startled crows. Good shot, but bad idea. He should have known that the only moisture in the whole patch would be in the barrel's belly. The ball was soaked in some foul-smelling goo. Benny bashed it against the wall a few times. Green smears marked the contacts.

Something scuttled behind a paint can. Benny saw just enough of the tail to realize it was a scorpion. He poked the can with his hurley. The scorpion sidestepped out for a look. Nasty-looking little chap with beady eyes and that big stinger arcing up over his head. They studied each other. The scorpion didn't look too scary. Barely bigger than the crawlies you'd catch on a beach at home. Still though, no point in taking chances. Benny hefted the hurley in a short grip and gave the unfortunate scorpion a good whack right on the crusty head. The insect cracked like an egg, green muck spurting through the gaps in his shell. Benny dug the hurley's blade under the smashed insect, lifting it on a little island of sand.

"Adios, my little poison buddy," he muttered and batted the scorpion over the wall.

The tennis ball was still a sopping blob. God knows what was in that sludge. Probably some universally banned chemical that was at this very moment chewing into the rubber at the center of his ball.

Something slapped into the back of his neck. It slid down his jersey, catching in the band of his shorts. After a moment of stark terror, he pulled the shirt up, flapping its tail around. The recently deceased scorpion dropped to the ground, its tail threatening even in death. Benny's first thought was as fleeting as it was dopey: the scorpion had come back to get him. No, not possible. That was one dead critter.

Benny got a prickly feeling between his shoulder blades. He knew, from years of being crept up on by hairy fullbacks, that there was someone behind him. Benny turned, and there he was. Perched on top of the perimeter wall with a cigarette hanging out of the corner of his mouth. A Tunisian lad, maybe eleven or twelve, flip-flops dangling from his toes. He pointed at the scorpion and then at his own leg. Must've hit him, thought Benny, without a whole lot of remorse.

"Just an accident, ye eejit," he shouted.

The boy smiled. More mocking than happy. His eyes and teeth stood out against caramel skin.

"Accident nine one one," he said. At least that's what Benny thought he said.

"What are you going on about?" challenged Benny, hoping for a bit of a confrontation.

The Tunisian's big Colgate grin widened. He rubbed his forehead, miming a huge lump.

"Tom and Jerry," he laughed, mimicking the unfortunate cat's face just after he got a whack of an ironing board.

"Oh, very humorous," snarled Benny. "You're a right laugh, you are." He made a mock run at the other boy, but he sat his ground. "Go off home to your goats!"

The Tunisian took a long pull on his cigarette, and then, with practiced accuracy, flicked the butt. It exploded on Benny's head in a shower of sparks. Yelping, he slapped at his hair. This his new enemy thought was a howl. He slapped his knees, laughing delightedly.

The legend of Cúchulainn stuffing his hurling ball down the throat of an attacking hound flashed back to the scalded Irish boy. He'd always thought he could fire one down someone's gullet. He'd found his victim. He retrieved the sopping ball and pulled with all the strength in his wiry arms. The chemical-soaked sphere bulleted through the air, trailing slime.

The Tunisian snatched it out of the air. Nodded his thanks. And was gone.

"What?" spluttered Benny. "Hey. C'mere, you! That's my ball!"

He knew what he should do. He should climb over that wall, puck the head off the kid and get his ball back. If Benny didn't go and get that ball, he might as well wear a T-shirt saying "Sucker" on it. Benny dropped the hurley and took a run at the wall. Too late, he changed his mind, ramming a shoulder into the concrete. This wasn't just an excursion into a hostile estate. The boy could be out there with his gang just waiting for the moron Irish boy. They could harvest his kidneys—or anything. Feeling utterly outsmarted, Benny trudged homeward. He gave the pool a wide berth; he'd had enough humiliation for one day.

When he came back after school the next day, the wall was still where he'd left it. Benny sucked the dregs from a carton of juice, then he batted the box over the wall, hoping for a reaction. Nothing. No little smart-aleck Arab leering down at him. It wasn't just pride at this stage, either. Their luggage hadn't arrived yet, so he was out of balls. Of course he'd been in the same clothes for the hottest three days of his life, too, but that wasn't bothering Benny yet. He'd gone two weeks in Cub Camp without a change of T-shirt. He wouldn't have changed his underpants either, if he hadn't fallen into the river.

He found a big pile of muck and concrete that ran halfway up the wall. Benny trudged up it, kicking his Reeboks through the crust like a mountain climber digging in spikes. He gave a quick bob over the rim, just in case that little chap had a blowpipe or something waiting. A hurried recon revealed no hostiles in the immediate vicinity.

A huge olive grove stretched off into the distance. Each tree was planted precisely on the corner of a ten-meter square. This sort of view went on uninterrupted for ages. Dust and pygmy trees. Charming.

Benny straddled the wall. Something was kicking around in the gravel beneath him. A couple of turkeys.

These were, without doubt, the skinniest birds that Benny had ever seen. There'd be no point in eating these lads; the only things covering their bandy bones were feathers. Except for the little wobbly bit under the beak, and even Benny balked at the idea of chewing on that. The wretched birds were tethered by blue string. Benny snorted. Like someone would steal these two! The string wound through the scrub back to a dingy-looking shack. A sheet of polythene was anchored over the structure by several red cinder blocks. The plastic was probably transparent back in the eighties, but now it was so daubed with mud and building smears that it was almost camouflaged.

There was no sign of the ballnapper. Benny listened for an evil villain's chortle. Nothing, except a few gobbles from the birds. Right, so here was the plan: hop down into the outside world, hurley raised to fend off animals or Zulus or whatever. Burst on over to the shelter in a rapid, but stealthy, fashion. Have a quick peek inside to judge the odds. If the little guy was there on his own, let a few roars and hopefully the kid would surrender the ball. If the shack had more than one occupant, he'd have to size them up and then settle on a course of action. Maybe they wouldn't have seen a white boy before and they'd treat him like some sort of god. Hardly likely though, based on the reactions of the Tunisians he'd already encountered.

Benny jumped from the wall. He was outside. In the

big bad world. Those birds seemed a lot bigger now. Their glittering eyes followed him like evil marbles.

"Back off, turkeys," he growled, trying to keep the falsetto from his voice. Onward, young man. Benny crept across the grove, clouds of dust rising with every footfall. He tiptoed around the perimeter, searching for an entrance. There wasn't one in the conventional sense, but there seemed to be a less solid bit on the village's blind side. Benny slapped the polythene with his hurley. No response.

"Come on, you little pirate!" he challenged with more bravado than he felt. "Come out and face the music."

Benny often wondered what was so desperate about facing music, though some of that seventies rock his da loved was fairly tortuous all right. Benny peered inside. Obviously nobody home. Thirty seconds, and he'd be in and out. It didn't feel exactly right breaking into someone's house. Ah, but what are you breaking? And was this a house?

Benny took a deep breath and slipped in. It was dark, and the sweet Tunisian smell was stronger than ever. You wouldn't know what would be in here, lurking. Maybe a trained scorpion or something. There were two pinpricks of light beaming at him from the darkness. Benny was on the verge of a reverse scuttle back to Marhaba when he realized that they were only pinpricks of light. Then something bonked against his head. Benny realized it was a lightbulb when he turned it on by accident.

This wasn't a bad little place. About the size of a storageroom but with a four-foot-high ceiling. The floor was covered with a patchwork layer of carpet remnants. The effect was spectacular: the patterns fused and striated to form a confusing jumble of color. If Ma saw this she'd probably want to run off and frame it. The walls and ceiling were lined with heavy cardboard boxes, bashed out to fit the corners. Your man even had appliances in here. There was a little fridge that hummed louder than the chalet's AC unit. And raised up in one corner was an old telly with a video recorder resting on it. Benny had a sneaking suspicion where the power came from to run this little hideaway.

It was obvious now that this place was the Tunisian lad's home, not just a lean-to for escaping the sun. A narrow mattress was pushed into one corner, piled high with blankets and glitzy cushions. And there, resting on the top cushion like a precious pearl, was the manky old tennis ball. Benny felt his manhood rushing back to him.

"Gotcha!" he hissed triumphantly, stuffing the ball down his shirt. All he had to do now was take a run at the wall and he was back on safe ground. Truth be told, he was feeling a bit shifty about being in someone else's house. Plus, for all he knew, the kid was the Chosen One of some fundamentalist group and might call for a religious jihad. It'd be just his luck to start a nationwide bloodbath. Da would tan his hide for sure.

He shuffled out, like a dog backing away from a fight. Pity he hadn't one of those Milk Tray man-in-black cards. That would learn the little Tunisian not to mess with a Yellowbelly from Wexford.

All these brave notions evaporated at the sound of an approaching engine. It sounded like a cross between a lawnmower and a narky wasp. Benny knew instantly that it was one of those moped things. He tumbled into the sunlight and saw that the little motorcycle was being driven by a sheep! The sheep looked as surprised as he was. Then Benny noticed two grimy brown hands poking out from beneath the animal's armpits. The helpless animal was a mere passenger, destined to join the rest of the roadside menagerie.

Benny scrambled to his feet, assessing his situation in a second. He'd been caught coming out of the Tunisian's house. Now, in the principal's office at home he might be able to talk his way out of that one, but here in Africa, all bets were off. You weren't given the civilized alternative of lying your face off to avoid trouble. There was him, your man and the wall. He could make a burst for it or he could stand his ground and trade pucks with the enemy. The sheep was too much. Benny went for the wall.

The boy jettisoned his bleating cargo and opened the throttle. Kicking up a stream of dust, the moped veered toward Benny. Benny sprinted flat out, slipping automatically into short breaths. The Tunisian bent low on his bike, determination pulling his lips back over his teeth. Benny lengthened his stride for the jump. Three steps and then up. He never figured on the turkey.

The bird appeared from behind a scut of a bush. Benny attempted a hop but so did the turkey. They collided in a flurry of feathers and scalded limbs. The bird got in a couple of good nips but Benny gave him a nice smack in the side of the head. Even with all this scuffling, Benny barely missed a step. He was well used to big hairy backs blindsiding him.

"I've eaten turkeys bigger than you," he scoffed, without a backward glance.

The whining motor was getting louder. Grit from the wheels smacked Benny on the legs. The Tunisian guy was shouting at him now. Indignant roars. There were only inches in it, but Benny was certain he could make it. He jumped. The moped's handlebars clipped his heels. Your man's forehead smacked into the hurley. Benny's wiry fingers scrabbled over the top. And he was up! Victorious. He looked back down for a bit of a gloat and his mood changed faster than a mackerel that's just realized that what he was chewing on wasn't a worm at all! The

Tunisian was off his bike, lying flat in the dust. There was a big red welt burning above his eyebrows. The moped was upended beside him, wheels whistling around unchecked. The menagerie had gathered in for a closer look, peering wide-eyed at their fallen master.

Oh God, thought Benny. He's dead. I killed him for a manky old tennis ball. Before he could get too emotional, the urchin stirred. Groaning mightily, he thrashed in the dust. Ah here! thought Benny, your man's looking for a penalty. His eyelids flickered open. Again they locked stares.

Ooops, thought Benny, fearing the worst. Maybe your man would break taboo and invade the village, assault him with that hurley . . . before that thought was even fully formed, Benny knew what had happened. He checked his right hand. There was nothing in it. That eejit must have head-butted it out of his grasp. A wave of nausea rippled through him. No, not the hurley! He smiled hopefully at the Tunisian boy. But only his teeth were smiling. The rest of him wanted to throw up.

The little dark fellow was on his feet now. He knew what he had. Benny's poker face was rubbish when it came to his hurley. Maybe your man would return it and they could develop a buddy-buddy, grudging respect type of friendship.

They all stared up at him, two turkeys, a sheep, and an

irate national. Daring him to come for the hurley. He wanted to do it. He was pretty certain he could take the boy and the turkeys, but the sheep was a wild card. Reluctantly, Benny remained astride the wall.

"Engine is fine," shouted the Tunisian.

Benny blinked. More English. This guy must watch a lot of telly.

"Engine is fine."

"Yeah, yeah. I heard you. Your engine's fine. So, gimme the hurley."

Benny held his hand out, flexing the fingers. In response the boy lifted the stick high over his head . . .

"No!" stammered Benny.

. . . and bashed it against the wall. He must be a strong little fellow because it cracked right across the center, bending like a boomerang.

Benny was in shock. His mouth flapped open. He had never been without a hurley. Never. This one had taken him months to break in. And took only a second to break.

The two boys looked at each other. The Tunisian was still belligerent, waving his trophy in the air.

"Engine is fine," he said again, but the backbone was gone out of it.

Benny wasn't even seeing him anymore. He was lost in his new future of hippie teachers, antiseptic kids, throbbing heat, mosquitoes, and no hurling. He slid off the wall, leaving his dusty enemy to his flip-flops and teth-ered animals. He was beaten. Eventually the Tunisian's indignant voice faded and Benny was alone in the aban-doned building site. He picked the tennis ball out of his jersey and threw it at the barrel. It didn't even get that far. Sure, what was the point of a ball on its own? Benny felt his throat rising up and he knew he was going to cry! Imagine, a fellow nearly in his teens crying over a hurley! The lads at home would buy tickets to see this. He coughed and shook his head, trying to stop it. But it was no good. The tears poured out of him, cleaning twin paths down his grimy cheeks.

The Tunisian boy's strange chant came back to him. It was clear now; your man wasn't talking about engines at all. What he was saying was: *vengeance is mine*. Fairly Biblical for a Muslim. Well, take your revenge and choke on it. The next time Benny Shaw would set foot outside that wall would be on the way home.

5
STICKY BONDY STUFF

The suitcases arrived on Friday, thank God. It was getting to the stage where you'd wash underwear and then sit around in a towel until it dried. Ma welcomed her make-up bag like a lost relative. The Crawler, of course, took his cue from her and went off the emotional deep end. He hugged each item passionately, tears of nostalgia pricking his eyes.

Benny was still being moody, and refused to be excited by anything. He just lolled around, smothered in a cock-tail of anti-mostique and Ambre Solaire.

School wasn't getting any better. This international curriculum they were doing did not link into Benny's own ideals on education. They couldn't even subtract right. They were doing something called renaming, instead of just carrying your ten. It made perfect sense to borrow ten from the top and pay it back at the bottom, remembering that a one could actually be a ten or a hundred depending on your column. But this crossing out a number lark was just ridiculous.

History and geography became social studies. Usually you could rely on those two. Same drill every year: Normans, Vikings, counties of Ireland. By the end of sixth year some of it would sink in. But Harmony was having none of that, even when Benny showed her his collection of "Norsemen on the rampage" pictures. Instead they were studying "The Making of the United Kingdom," something Benny wouldn't be letting on about to Father Barty when he got home. And "Ecological Disasters of the Twentieth Century." Benny felt cheated. He'd learned the map of Ireland in second class and thought that would see him through secondary.

PE was the pits. Here, at least, Benny thought he could shine. Whatever the sport was, there was no doubt he could stuff these other kids. Harmony, however, didn't believe in competition. She said it turned our focus outward instead of inward. So instead they did aerobics and fitness exercises. When they did eventually get to play a game of rounders, or rather, softball, everyone encouraged the other team and let the little kiddies steal home. It was disgusting.

Grace, the Scottish girl, walked home with him after school. They were silent, each waiting for the other to speak. The heat was belting off Benny and flies kept getting foul hooked in his cowlick.

"Well . . ." said Grace, dry and insect free.

"Well . . ." said Benny, batting at a particularly persistent mosquito.

"So, are you planning to talk to anybody?"

"Huh?"

"Socially, you know, apart from smart comments during Missus Rossi's . . . Harmony's class."

"Aha!" gloated Benny. "You find the first-name thing a bit off too."

"I did," admitted Grace. "Old habits die hard. But I kind of like it now. It just takes time, you see. Anyway, are you coming to the barbecue?"

"Dunno. Am I asked?"

Grace elbowed him. "Stop it."

"Okay. I suppose so. Just the older kids, is it?"

"And the adults."

"Righto."

"Maybe you can actually talk to Zoe and the rest without being smart."

Benny shrugged. "I don't know. I wouldn't put money on it. I mean, Scottish is one thing. But Americans—I don't know."

"C'mon, Benny. Be nice."

"I'll try, but the way my luck's been going, I can't promise."

* * *

Grace's folks, the Tafts, had really made the effort for this barbecue. Their patio was all done out in fairy lights. Two speakers were perched on the wall, pumping out the always trendy "Beautiful South." Plastic tables were dotted around the surrounding green, unsteady on the springy grass. Beer cans floated in ice-packed coolers. Mr. Taft was behind a large gas barbecue, trying to make a dent in a huge platter of chicken. He wore shorts and a tartan apron.

"Thirsty work, Stuart," said Da, handing him a Guinness.

Stuart Taft rolled the cool can along his forehead. "Go on, you beauty," he smiled. "This stuff is liquid gold here. The local brew is a bit unreliable. Practically glows in the dark."

They popped their cans and drank deeply. Instant buddies.

"This is Jessica, my wife."

Stuart Taft glanced up and nodded. Then his brain registered what he had seen and his smile cranked open almost to his ears.

"Well hello, Jessica. Would you like a glass of wine?"

"That would be delightful, Stuart."

Stuart bustled off, cutting a swath through the crowd; Jessica often had that effect on men. Something about her red curly hair and freckled colleen's complexion. Da always got a chuckle out of it. It made Benny want to barf. He wandered off to inspect the insect coil. Various flying things had collided with the mesh, lured into electrocution by the pretty purple light.

"Hey, Benny." It was Grace. She had a polka-dot dress on. It looked nice.

"You look nice," he said. Just like that, it slipped out. Three words that would forever brand him as a simpering eejit. He tried to salvage the situation. "That fly frier is a handy gadget," he commented pleasantly.

Grace nodded.

"Turns 'em into flying cinders," continued Benny blithely.

The Scottish girl's grin faltered. "I suppose it does."

"A few of 'em probably just get singed on one wing and then spend the rest of their lives buzzing around in circles." He knew he was digging himself in deeper but he couldn't help it. "I don't usually think about flies gettin' mutilated. Or any insects really. I just sort of got on this subject and I can't get off."

Grace smiled. "It's fine, Benny. Just take it easy. Here, have a Coke."

"Thanks."

Grace pointed at a table. "We're all over here," she said.

Willing himself not to sweat, Benny followed her over.

Heather and Ed were grinning over huge paper cups. Zoe was immersed in some sort of chocolate-stuffed banana. Benny would've liked to ask about it, but expressing an interest in desserts was not cool. James was destroying a plate of chicken with greasy efficiency. He spared Benny an eyebrow wiggle of greeting.

"Howyez," said Benny, suddenly realizing that he smelled like a sachet of Lemsip from all the insect repellant he'd plastered on. There was an empty seat beside Grace. He took it. Now what?

"Stop staring at me, lads. You're making me nervous."

Zoe splurted out a mouthful of brown banana mush. "C'mon, Benny boy. You're the one making everyone, like, nervous."

Benny blinked. "Me?" He looked to Grace for support.

"It's true, Benny. Every time you open your mouth it's to tease someone."

"It is not."

Ed and Heather nodded over their cups.

"Gang up on me, why don't you?" muttered Benny.

Grace sighed. "Here we go again."

Benny opened his mouth to object but couldn't. For a split second, he grasped how simple it would be for him to fit in. All he had to do was to accept everyone here at face value. No more smart aleckry, just be nice for a change. His brain was about to unfold this revelation, when he noticed a mosquito straddling his shinbone.

He hopped up like a jack-in-the-box, catching his knobbly knees on the rim of the table. It spun up like a Frisbee, splashing its contents all over Grace. It shouldn't have happened that way. The laws of physics dictated that the food be equally distributed, but Murphy's Law intervened and dumped two pints of Coke, half a chicken, and a chocolate banana on the unfortunate girl's new dress.

"That's, like, too much, Benny," said Zoe.

"Yeah, enough is enough," added Ed.

"But I——" protested Benny.

"We know," said Heather. "That's the way you do things at home."

Benny looked to Grace. Surely she could see it was a big, stupid, clumsy accident. But Grace was the cruellest of all—she was sobbing gently into a *Lion King* napkin.

Benny began to sweat. He felt like his feet were swimming in his Reeboks. "Listen, Grace——"

"Just leave us alone," interjected Heather, on a roll now. "We're fed up trying to be nice to you. Some of us never wanted to in the first place."

Later, when Benny thought about it, he liked to think that he exited with some dignity. The pathetic truth was that he bolted off like Georgie in one of his prima donna sulks.

That's it, thought Benny. This country isn't getting any

more chances. He'd done his bit, opened himself to new experiences. But this latest episode was the straw that broke the camel's back. Pretty funny, that. Seeing as he was in the land of camels.

The front door was before him. Beyond it was George. And wouldn't the Crawler just love this? Benny raised his hand to the door handle. His fingers brushed something wooden and knocked it to the grass. He recognized the touch of the grain immediately. Benny sank to his knees like the knight who found the holy grail.

It was his hurley. Back from the dead. And in one piece. Benny was dumbfounded. How could this be? Once you broke a stick over someone's shinguards, that was that. Benny balanced it on one finger, testing for weight. It was as close as made no difference. There was a layer of some sort of sticky, bondy stuff around the shaft. Like plaster of paris or something, only sanded and varnished. He gave it a swing. The whistle was a bit different, must be a few sloppy edges catching the air. He leaned it on the angle of the wall and put his knee into the center. A good spring but no crack. This was primo work, you had to admit it. But whose work?

The EuroGas flare was flaming up to the stars, dwarfing even the city lights. Benny squinted into the night, trying to see the little Tunisian fellow's hut. After a while, he thought he could make out a dark bump on the ground beneath him.

If you asked Benny precisely what he was doing straddling the perimeter wall of a guarded African camp, he wouldn't have been able to tell you exactly. Simple human curiosity. He had to find out what his new enemy, or friend, or whatever, was playing at. Maybe he'd just hop down and give the side of his domicile a little nudge. See what developed. It was a sort of open-ended plan. A good strong beginning, but fairly feeble toward the end. Still, Benny was dropping to the ground as soon as the idea occurred to him. Father Barty had two theories about Benny's impulsiveness. If he scored, then he had great instincts. If not, then he was a fool who never thought things through. His sneakers crunched on the gravel. He stayed crouched for a moment, listening for movement.

It seemed that the night was suddenly filled with noises he hadn't noticed before. The dogs were out in force, howling away goodo. There were sheep going, too. Probably being chased by the dogs. Insects were clicking and whistling, getting set for a night of scavenging or bloodsucking. It was just like a Tarzan movie. At last, Africa was starting to sound the way the telly said it should.

Benny heard something behind him. He spun around, nearly tripping over his own laces. A red dot was glowing in the blackness by the wall. Someone was having a sly smoke. The red tip bobbed up two feet and then came out from the lee of the wall. It was, of course, his good buddy, whatever his name was.

"*Marhaba,*" said the boy.

"I don't speak Tunisian," replied Benny.

"*Marhaba,*" repeated the boy emphatically.

"I don't speak Tunisian," shouted Benny, gesticulating elaborately.

The boy took a final drag from his cigarette and then flicked it into the bush. An indignant turkey bolted off, flapping one of its wings. After a moment's thought, the boy said, "Welcome to Sherwood."

Here we go, thought Benny, a genuine nutcase. "Thank you," he waved the hurley. "Thank you . . . ah . . . *merci . . . shokran.*"

The boy smiled. Big white teeth gleamed, giving him a face like a kid instead of a little adult.

"The name's Bond," he lilted. "James Bond Omar."

English by satellite stations. Who said telly wasn't educational?

"Omar?"

"*Na'am.*"

"Okay. My name's . . . The name's Bond. James Bond Benny."

"Binny?"

"No, Benny. Ben-nee."

"Benny?"

"Yes . . . ah . . . *Na'am*."

This tickled Omar no end. "*Na'am*, Benny, *na'am, na'am*."

Benny took a close look at the strange boy. He was a far cry from the usual romantic image conjured up by the name Omar. He wore battered loafers, once-white sports socks, and a gray tracksuit covered with layers of jumpers and shorts. His head seemed small compared to his padded body. Black curly hair trickled down over a wide brow and black eyes. His cheeks were sharp and hungry looking, and he had a set of teeth that went all the way out to his ears.

"Sorry about the house," said Benny.

Omar shrugged.

"The house." Benny pointed to where he thought the shack was.

"Ah . . ." said Omar, realization broadening his smile. "B and E. Mandatory three to five."

Benny laughed. It was like himself speaking Irish. Go for gist rather than accuracy.

They stood staring at each other like a couple of fools.

"Nice job on the hurley," said Benny rubbing the shaft. He whacked the hurley on the ground. "Good and strong."

Omar nodded wisely. "Super glue. Bonds in seconds. Lasts an eternity."

Benny blinked. He wondered if he actually had used super glue, or if that was just the handiest ad. The little moped was propped against a prickly-pear bush. "Bike's okay, then, eh, Omar?"

Omar spat on the petrol tank and rubbed off a spot of dust. Not just a pretend spit either. This was a big glob of bubbles and water. Benny thought that he'd spit too, if he had a moped like this one. The bike suited Omar perfectly. Like his outfit, it seemed to have been assembled from the wrecks of various others. It was not a bike you'd sit at home with and polish. This was a machine that earned its keep.

"Chips?" said Omar, swinging a leg over the seat.

"Excusez-moi?" Benny knew that much at least.

The Tunisian screwed another cigarette between his lips. "CHIPS," he repeated. "Omar Ponch, Binny Jon."

"That's Benny."

"Benny . . . Jon."

The memory of an often repeated California Highway Patrol series filtered through years of rainy Saturday morning telly sessions.

"So you want me to hop on the back and go for a spin around?"

Benny realized that he was talking to himself. Omar didn't speak English, only TV.

"Ah . . . Omar, Benny—*broom broom*." Benny made what he hoped were throttle-opening movements with his hands.

"Holy moley, you've got it, Batman," grinned Omar.

Dilemma time for Benny. There was nothing he would like better than to jump on this machine and hare around the desert. It was only natural. He was male and it could go faster than him. But it was BAD. He knew that if his ma got one peek at this bike, she would absolutely order him not to go anywhere near it. Omar was giving him that uncertain, I hope I haven't befriended a chicken look. Tough call.

"You know you're getting me in trouble here, shorty. If I'm caught sitting on that thing, I'll never sit down again."

Omar gave him a thumbs-up sign, pulling the moped erect. He pedalled to start. The engine growled into life, sending revs vibrating across the dirt. Benny shivered. How could any boy be expected to resist something like that?

"Okay, then," he grunted, as if he was doing Omar a favor. He approached the little Peugeot warily, taking a good look at what he was entrusting his life to. The bike was rattling like an old plumbing system. Big wet lumps of smoke were toppling out of her exhaust. The original paintwork had long since been blasted off by African winds. It was replaced by primer, emulsion, and what looked like nail varnish. The seat was a cracked velour; tufts of burned foam peeked out from split seams. The sweat of a thousand close calls had done their damage. Omar rubbed the handlebars fondly. And he was right. She was beautiful.

Benny climbed onto the shuddering machine. Suddenly he had to shout to be heard. "Just around here, all right? *Ici*," he roared, wishing he knew the international code sign for "Don't go on the road."

Omar nodded and opened her up. Turkeys dived for their lives and Benny realized neither Omar nor he had a helmet. The back wheel slewed sideways, searching for purchase—it probably wouldn't do that if there was any tread on the rubber!

They moved at what seemed like warp speed. Dust maelstroms swam in the red rear light. Omar was roaring with laughter. Benny found himself joining in. You couldn't help it. It felt like a rollercoaster ride, only more dangerous. The lights of Marhaba village receded behind them and Benny waited for Omar to hang some kind of spectacular turn, digging a circular skid mark into the dirt. He didn't. Benny tapped his new friend on the shoulder, waving his finger in a circular motion. Omar must have translated this into "open her up" because he leaned into the wind and twisted his wrist way back. They sprang forward like they were on elastic. For a second the jarring stopped and they seemed to be flying. Benny squinted through the dust and insects. The ground was gone. It came back with a thump. But now it was black. They were on the road. Benny swallowed. It looked like they were going for a spin into town.

6

SPLITTING
INTERNAL ORGANS

Benny was trying to remember what in the name of sanity had induced him to climb on the back of this death machine. He couldn't. The night was dark, the road was black, and Omar appeared to have turned his lights off. Logic tried to tell Benny that they could only be doing about twenty miles an hour, but his logic circuits were burnt out at this stage.

They bounced along the narrow tarmac strip, attempting to land at least one wheel in every pothole along the way. Each jolt threatened to spill the pair from their seats. Benny felt as though his internal organs were being shaken loose. There was no footpath on the verge, just a jagged six-inch drop to the sand. One slipup at this speed, and you'd be sailing, bum first, into the darkness. Shadowy prickly pears lurked like muggers in the fields, waiting for some poor Irishman to somersault into their stiletto clutches.

They were approaching the railway crossing. Benny tried to remember what your man Khayssi had told them about that. Something about not being reliable. He took a breath to tell Omar—and a big, buzzy, wingy bug darted right down his gullet. By the time he'd coughed it and half the lining of his throat all over Omar's sweatshirt, they were past the level crossing and bombing toward the suburbs.

Omar threw a long skidder onto the Tyna Road. The moped missed a few strokes and then kicked in with a terrific backfire. They were immediately immersed in general population. After a few minutes, Benny opened his eyes. They were careering down a two-lane road, and traffic was bad. Four-wheelers chugged along, hindered by the lights and congestion. And through it all, the mopeds flowed like goldfish in a sea of sharks. The road was lined with squat, flat-roofed buildings. Swarthy-looking men sat outside cafés in droves, glaring balefully at the passing traffic. You could cast a right few pirate movies with this lot. Drooping moustaches and all.

In moments they were off the tarmac, and Omar cut left on to one half of a set of huge tire tracks. The surface was like sand, only flakier. Walls of gray dust loomed on either side. Benny had no idea what sort of a place he was in. The old nagging worries started to kick in again. Maybe this kid was bringing him out here for a spot of human sacrifice, or a little white-slavery deal.

They were in a huge flat area, maybe twice the size of Croke Park. The moonlight gave it a spooky glow, and it loomed over the town like an avalanche waiting to happen. Omar, of course, roared right into the center, kicking up a ten-foot-high wave of dust in his wake. He tried for a long circular skid, but the weight was too much for the little Peugeot. The two boys tumbled off, rolling across the compacted dust. They came up coated and spitting. Omar spread his arms wide. "Wembley Stadium," he grinned, his teeth like landing lights.

"Wembley Stadium!" snorted Benny. "This is some chemical heap. God knows what we're swallowing here."

Omar jumped up undaunted, leaving the conked-out bike where it was. He ran in a wide circle, barking like an eejit. Instantly, a pack of mongrels howled in reply. Benny swallowed. Those dogs sounded close. Omar flopped breathless onto the ground. Covered in dust like he was, he looked like a happy corpse.

"Short commercial break," he gasped. "Then the game begins."

"Game? What game? Sure, it's pitch black."

Omar, who still couldn't speak English, ignored the Irish cynic. Gazing up at the stars, he clamped a cigarette between his molars.

Benny plucked it out and threw it away. "They'll kill you," he said.

Omar scrabbled through the dust, finding and brushing off his cigarette.

"Bad!" said Benny pointing. "Cough, cough, cancer and all that." He did a choking mime and then collapsed dramatically, clutching his heart.

Omar didn't smile. Instead he looked thoughtful. Da got that look when he was bending over a spreadsheet late at night. Benny gave him an interrogative eyebrow wiggle.

Omar concentrated. "Smoking can damage your unborn baby," he said finally.

Benny nodded. Fair enough.

Then Omar did a strange thing. He kicked his heel through the crust on the slag heap and pulled out a fistful of dust. It stank and there was the odd bit of slime laced through it. He threw it high into the air and the breeze stuck it right back in his face. Omar smiled sadly and shrugged. The shrug said: What's the point? What's the point of giving up the cigarettes when you were breathing in this pollutant every day?

The dogs were getting closer. Omar cocked an ear to the wind and returned their cry.

"Oh, that's great, Omar, boy," muttered Benny. "Sure, call in the dogs, why don't you?"

The dogs came, but they came on mopeds. Bursting through from another path carved into the monstrous pilings heap, they erupted on to the flat crust, spewing dust like some western posse. Benny squared off. Well, how were you supposed to react to young fellas who called a get-together by howling like kicked pups?

"The Merry Men," said Omar happily.

Benny was starting to feel extremely outnumbered. Like the time six muckers from the Brothers' team had caught him in the square. He still had a fleshy ridge on the top of his head from that one.

They pulled in on four bikes, each one loaded down to the mudguards. A dozen or so lads hopped off and instantly started a big wrestling match on the ground. Hopefully this was a friendly tussle and not some inter-tribal vendetta.

Omar emerged from a gap in the heap, grinning all over his face. Benny's new friend threw a few kicks into the bunch until they let go of each other. Laughing and spitting, they shuffled into a ragged line and began to pick teams. Teams for what, wondered Benny? They'd no ball, no goals, and no light. Plus, they all looked identical, covered in that gray stuff. He realized suddenly why they weren't paying him much attention. He was layered in dust, too. In this light he probably looked exactly like one of them. Good. Anonymity suited Benny just fine.

Omar dragged him forward by the arm. Slapping dust from Benny's head, he explained something in Arabic to his cohorts. Everybody suddenly became very interested.

Here's where the bidding starts, thought Benny, though judging by the state of this crowd, they hadn't the price of a bag of Taytos between them. He nodded and grinned, the image of a friendly visitor.

"Howyez, lads," he said. "Any sudden moves and I belt the heads off ye."

The Tunisians were extremely interested in his Reeboks. One of them actually dropped to his knees for a squint.

"That's the real thing. None of your Ruuboks or Air Johnson," said Benny.

Omar tolerated this hogging of his new friend for a while, then he booted the foot inspector in the backside and claimed Benny for his team.

"What?" asked Benny. "Are we going to hurl insults or what?"

"Soccer," said Omar. "Premier league with Andy Gray."

"Soccer!" said Benny. "But I'm rubbish at soccer."

Omar dragged him on, undaunted. The boys were pairing off, throwing down jerseys for goalposts. Another fellow hared off with a stick, scratching lines through the crust. He soon disappeared into the night.

"Sure, look," squeaked Benny, "I can't even see that chap marking the pitch."

Unfortunately, Omar had no clue what he was saying.

"Ahm . . . after dark . . . sun, no sun," Benny tried.

Omar laughed, clapping him on the back. "Binny!"

"That's Benny."

"*Na'am, na'am.* Benny." Omar pointed up ahead. "Kellogg's Cornflakes: the sunshine breakfast."

Benny's gaze followed Omar's finger: finally, thought Benny, a hand with more scabs than his. Grace should get a look at this guy. She might appreciate himself a bit more. Eventually Benny got past this and actually looked where Omar was pointing.

"What? A big black hole."

Something rumbled. A deep growly roar. Benny felt a vibration ripple through his soles. "Oh no! It's a lion," he gasped, raising his hurley high.

Omar understood "lion," probably had seen it on a Disney video or something. He laughed so hard that he nearly threw up his lungs. In fractious sentences he explained Benny's remark to the rest of the Dog Squad. They howled so much that they all had to sit down and have a cigarette.

"Laugh it up, smart alecks. I hope Simba comes out of them shadows and bites the smiley heads off you."

Omar wiped his nose with great gusto and draped a sympathetic arm around the poor Irish eejit's shoulders.

"The sunshine breakfast," said Omar again, and the light came on.

Benny recognized the smell of diesel. It was a digger. A big, rubber wheeled, yellow digger. A huge spotlight squatted on the cab.

"The sun has got its hat on," said Omar.

"Oh, shut your face," said Benny, but he couldn't help smiling. When you had a group of lads looking for a game, anything was possible.

So it was six opposite six. Benny got a decent look at his teammates from his place in goal. The harsh light made them look like moving statues. Someone produced an old burst ball wrapped in masking tape and they were off. As with all things Tunisian, nothing proceeded without argument.

The boys fouled each other and performed spectacular dives. While they were arguing about that, some sneaky little chap would nip up the wing and score in an open goal. Then a whole new row would erupt. After a while, they got four or five arguments behind, and everybody was roaring at cross purposes. Some of the guys got so bored they even fired up some more cigarettes.

Benny was just starting to doze off when the first shot blurred past him. He didn't see it or anything, it just clipped his elbow on the way in. He yelped. These lads could certainly move when they felt like it. It was real Brazilian-boys-in-the-ghetto type of stuff. Burst ball and bare feet, attempting all sorts of high-flying gymnastics. They were doing overheads, benders, and diving headers. No wonder some of these boys had flat foreheads and dopey stares. Sure that must be like nutting a lump of rock.

Omar, of course, was in the thick of it, handling that solid little ball like it was a balloon. They could have notched up about four or five hundred goals, but it was much more important to score with style than just belt one past the goalie. Passing was definitely optional. Every man jack of them was determined to go from one end of the "pitch" to the other and then have a go in some acrobatic fashion. A fair few of them managed it too. Benny had no chance.

After a while it started to get embarrassing. There was this one lad in particular. A big gangly chap with a notice-able absence of front teeth. He'd bull his way through, and slide the ball past Benny with the side of his foot. Then, grinning gummily, he'd belly slide through the dust for ten or fifteen yards. Har-de-har-har, thought Benny. Like he'd come three thousand miles to be humiliated.

As if that wasn't bad enough, they started throwing him dummies. Pulling their feet way back and then tap-ping it between Benny's legs. Benny could feel the heat of his embarrassment fusing the phosphate dust to his face. Then came the ultimate: the lowest of the low that has all sportsmen contemplating hara-kiri. The Tunisians took pity on him! They started tapping in pitiful little shots and being theatrically disgusted when the Irish boy saved them. For an instant, Benny realized why some people didn't like sports. If you weren't good, it was no fun whatsoever.

Omar trotted back every now and then to give his new friend a quick thumbs-up before disappearing back into the mêlée. Benny smiled sarcastically to convey what an absolutely brilliant time he wasn't having. Unfortunately, underneath the camouflage, all Omar could see was teeth. Teeth equalled happiness. Okeydokey.

Eventually it seemed to come down to penalties, probably because not a soul there had any clue what the score was. Benny was glad of the rest while the other goalie sweated it out. Even standing up was doing him in. Omar strolled over, yet another cigarette glowing between his teeth. Benny hoped the chemical slag wasn't flammable.

"*Mabrook,*" he said enthusiastically.

"Yeah, yeah, right," said Benny, He knew that tone. He'd used it himself to patronize a hundred waster goalies.

Omar threw an arm over Benny's shoulder, leading him to the makeshift sideline. Obviously Benny was meant to sit this one out. Taken off when the pressure was on. Oh, the shame.

"Hold your horses, there," said Benny, stomping back

to the goal. "If I'm good enough for the beginning, I'm good enough for the end." If Father Barty could hear him now, fighting to stay on a soccer pitch. He grabbed his hurley from the pile of jerseys. "Okay if I use this?"

Omar grimaced. He didn't really want to offend his new friend. But how were you supposed to stop a football with a stick? Plus, he was going to have to propose this plan to his buddies. He did. They laughed. Well, laughed was a bit of a tame word, really. It was quite possible that a few of them split internal organs.

"Yuck it up, boys," said Benny, his confidence returning with the touch of the wood. Naturally, it was old gap-tooth who came to take the shot. He gave Benny a wiggly fingered wave, in case he had forgotten him.

Benny planted his feet wide and put the hurley across his knees. "Go between me legs," he said. "I dare ye."

The Tunisian took a few steps back. He plucked his cigarette from his mouth where it had been wedged between two widely spaced teeth. Tossing it to the dirt, he casually ground it beneath a naked foot.

Benny winced. Everybody did—including the lanky fellow himself. You're going to have a lovely blister there tomorrow, thought Benny. The price of being hard.

Gummy took a running smack at the little ball. Now that Benny had the hurley in his hand, the save seemed ridiculously easy. He tipped the ball upward, holding it there with its own spin. Glancing briefly at the other goal, he gently nudged the spinning ball higher into the air and whacked it with every last iota of strength in his wiry arms. Your man, the other goalie, just got out of the way. Back of the net. If there had been a net. Benny smiled. Pick the bones out of that one. Vindication at last. Omar howled and hugged Benny, swinging him off the ground. That was soccer players for you.

Gummy immediately lodged an official complaint and the arguing began again. Benny knew the law was against him. There was no way that you could score from the line during a penalty shoot-out. But knowing these lads' love of flair, they would probably let it stand.

And they did. Sure, you couldn't disqualify a goal like that. Now they all wanted a look at the hurley. Then a smack of the ball. Seeing these chaps swinging like eejits and not hitting a thing took Benny back to when he was four. It was funny how you could go from being a nerd to cool in the space of two seconds.

Someone produced a black plastic bag and shared around loaves of pita bread. They tore off hunks and drank cloudy water from an old Coke bottle. Benny knew full well that he wasn't supposed to be drinking mystery water, and there was a good chance that some part of his body would pay the price. He even made an attempt to refuse the bottle but the boys were having none of it. And to seal the deal, it was Gummy who offered it to him. How could he say no to that chap after turning his own shot against him?

It occurred to Benny that he hadn't been this happy since leaving Ireland.

Omar dropped him back at the wall. The two of them perched on top, watching the glow from the EuroGas plant.

"Where's your family, Omar?" asked Benny. Then he tried to convert it to television-speak. "Ah . . . Homer Simpson?"

Omar nodded. "Doh!" he said, slapping his forehead.

"Okay . . . You Bart. Homer and Marge?"

The Tunisian boy computed this. "No Homer. No Marge." He looked suddenly sad. Benny was sorry he'd asked. Omar pointed down toward the railway crossing. A triangle of green lights was the only illumination on the Gabes Road.

He took a long breath. "Homer, Marge: Thomas the Tank Engine—boom."

Benny swallowed. Being Tunisian wasn't easy. Having a moped suddenly didn't seem like all that much of a plus. Benny didn't know what to say. And even if he had, he couldn't have translated it.

"Lisa," said Omar.

"Huh?"

"Homer, Marge—boom. Lisa: casualty, Chicago Hope."

So there was a sister. Somewhere in a hospital. Of course, he could be totally misinterpreting everything this strange little chap said. Benny glanced over his shoulder. The fairy lights were still on in the Tafts' yard. Maybe there was a chance he could make it in before Ma and Da.

"*Bonzwar*, Omar," he said, dropping back into Marhaba village. "I have to head before the parents make it home."

"*Bonsoir*, Binny," replied Omar. "Join us again tomorrow . . ."

"Same time, same channel," completed Benny. He was starting to get the hang of this.

7
THIS TIME, IT'S PERSONAL

And just as Benny was starting to feel human again, just as he was contemplating all sorts of dinky little plans, the water that he shouldn't have drunk came back to say hello. Now, luckily for Benny he didn't get malaria or any other serious disease. What he did get was a long and painful attack of . . . well, let's just say it was a good job he was already in the bathroom.

Benny didn't venture out again until Sunday. And even then, between the stiffness and his recent affliction, he was feeling a bit delicate. The weather, as usual, was scorching. Not a cloud in the aquamarine sky. Benny was reminded of one of those spaghetti westerns where Clint Eastwood squints through the rippling heat at whatever chap he's about to ventilate. Benny took a slug from his water bottle. He'd decided it might be healthier to carry his own supply from now on. He was hoping to make it over the wall without bumping into anyone. Firstly, because his system wasn't ready for any bumping just yet. Secondly, because a high percentage of Marhaba village's occupants wanted his head on a spike.

He needn't have worried. The families were all occupied watching a soccer game. Soccer again. There was no getting away from it. Grace's da was playing. Even Pat Shaw had been nabbed and stood, looking fairly sheepish, in a EuroGas jersey. Jessica was supporting from the sidelines. The kids were grouped around the line. Unlike normal children who shunned any activity that involved their parents, the girls had actually made pompoms to cheer on their daddies. The family-outing feel was completed by trays of barbecued chicken and chocolate cheesecake sitting on shaded tables.

Benny squinted. Something was shining in his eyes. He traced the source of the glare. Mohamed Gama was glaring at him. The sunlight was reflecting on his bald head. Benny ducked below the beam.

"Hey, Gama, get a cap," he shouted across at the guard. "Don't dazzle. Dip!"

He got no response except the by-now-expected scowl. Benny strolled to the old building site. Nobody watched him go.

There was half a set of steps, a wooden frame keeled over on the ground, a jagged line of blocks, a slalom of steel rods, and, of course, the barrel. Benny spun the discolored tennis ball on to his hurley. He took a deep breath and ran, letting the stick dangle low to the ground. He went up the steps, through the frame, zigzagged around the rods, and for the big finish, belted the ball into the barrel. Rust flakes fluttered in a victory shower.

"Good on ye, boy," whooped Benny, the sweat pumping out of him. But then he remembered the All-Ireland Final and was instantly depressed again. This time next week, Wexford would be playing in the most important match ever—and he'd be stuck in Africa watching his Da play soccer.

A slow clap interrupted his impending sulk. Omar was sitting on the wall, applauding his little obstacle course.

"Howzagoin', Omar?"

"*Kif halek*, Binny?"

"That's Benny."

Omar glanced around furtively and hopped on to the cement pile. He nodded at the hurley.

Benny smiled. "You're going to have to ask for it, Omar, boy."

Omar held out his hand, wiggling the fingers.

"Got an itchy hand, have you?"

Omar scowled. "Ah . . . need a loan, call the experts."

"Oh, you want a loan. Of what?"

That was too much for Omar. He bulled in, head

down. But Benny was well used to this. He sidestepped and gave Omar's rear end a clip on its way past.

"Hurley," he said, waving the stick.

"Hu-relly."

"No, eejit. Hurley."

"Hurley eejit."

You had to laugh. So Benny did.

"Here, go on," he said, passing over the hurley. "You have to go up the steps, through that frame, round the rods."

Omar nodded earnestly, following the finger. "*Na'am*," he said.

"Oh look at you. It's not an axe, you know."

"Axe you know."

"Go on—you're only a parrot."

"Eejit," said Omar slyly.

Shaking his head in mock despair, Benny tried to show Omar the proper grip.

"Y'see, you put your strong hand on the end, see. Here. That's right. And the other hand over it. Good man."

Omar took the ball and placed it on the hurley. It fell off.

Benny gave him a clap. "Oh, good man. Well done."

Omar growled. He tried it again. No luck. Spitting a stream of what sounded like vile Arabic, the Tunisian boy threw the ball and stick to the ground. "Bad," he snapped. "Lex Luthor. Ordinary cleaners."

"Oh right," scoffed Benny. "Bad hurley. Bad ball."

"Eejit!"

"Watch it, you." Benny retrieved the discarded implements and began carelessly bouncing the ball on the hurley. "Oh this is difficult! It's so tough I may cry like a ballerina."

Omar tried another attack, and this time Benny wasn't fast enough. They went down in a heap, scuffling like two bear cubs. Omar was a small chap but he fought like a cornered badger. Eventually Benny pinned him.

"Halftime," he panted.

"Commercial break," agreed Omar.

He headed for the wall, motioning for Benny to follow. Benny climbed the mound warily. "Omar, no Wembley Stadium?"

"*Na'am*."

"What's that? *Na'am*, yes: no Wembley Stadium, or *na'am*, no: no Wembley Stadium?"

Omar was justifiably confused. And would have been even if he had spoken English.

"*Mafi* Wembley," said Omar, shaking his head.

So *mafi* was negative. File and store.

"*Très bien*," said Benny. Harmony would be proud of him.

Omar kicked a turkey out of the way. "*Mafi* Wembley," he continued. "Today's lineup, Tetley's."

"What?"

"Tetley's. Ooh in Typhoo. The taste of ground coffee without the grind."

"*Na'am*, Omar boy." Obviously it was beverage time.

They ducked into the shack. The place was like an oven. Omar pulled a fan out and plugged it into a chipped socket strip. After a few sparks, the motor caught and the battered blades hummed into life.

"That's a grand breeze there."

Omar nodded. "Foster's Ice," he said, rummaging on his shelves for glasses.

Benny spotted a TV guide rolled under the VCR. His heart lurched but then calmed. There was no chance. But he pulled it out anyway. This month's. Don't even hope. You're in Africa. With clumsy fingers he flicked open to the listings. Last Sunday in August. Eurosport—tennis, skiing, tractor pulling. Benny was disgusted. Tractor pulling, for God's sake! And they wouldn't put on the most important game in the universe. He scanned the other sports channels and passed the match listing before he realized it. Hold it, his brain said. Back 'er up there a bit. He did so. Sky Sports Three. Three P.M. GMT, whatever that was, live coverage of the All-Ireland Hurling Final! Sky Three. He pushed the magazine into Omar's face.

"Omar! Have you got this station?"

Blank.

"Ah . . . television?"

"*Na'am.*"

"Sky . . . BBC . . . MTV?"

Omar copped on fast. "Eurosport . . . CNN . . . NBC . . ."

"Yes. That's it! *Na'am.* So, have you got Sky?"

"Sky?"

"Sky! Sky!" Benny was losing it. He pointed at the program. "Look here, Omar, y'eejit."

"Eejit, Binny."

"Okay . . . Look now. Right here. Three o'clock. All-Ireland Final."

"No Englese?"

No wonder they thought he'd be able to play soccer. "No Engleezee. I'm . . . Ah . . . Irelandeezi."

"Oh!"

"Omar! Sky Three."

The Tunisian boy followed the finger, finally getting the message. "Ah! Skee!"

"Sky, Ski. Whatever."

Omar shook his head. The kiss of death. "*Mafi* Skee."

Benny knew it was true. They didn't get it in the village either. So it was hardly likely that Omar here would pick it up on his pirated system. Especially since the signal was probably robbed from Marhaba.

"*Mafi* Skee *ici.*" Now Omar was trilingual! "Tunis Skee!"

"Yeah, whatever." Benny had no interest anymore.

But Omar decided a demonstration was necessary. He switched on the battered TV. "Binny," he said grandly, pointing at the screen. "NBC."

All Benny could see was static.

Omar shrieked like a sow who'd lost her piglets. Frantically he flicked through the channels. Nothing. All snowstorms. Omar was devastated. He scrolled through the stations. Again and again. Eventually Benny had to pry the remote from between his fingers.

"Calm down there, young lad. It's only television."

"*Mafi* TV," Omar croaked.

"Don't talk to me. *Mafi* All-Ireland either."

Omar's eyes narrowed to slits. "Gama!" he hissed.

"What? Mohamed Gama?"

"*Na'am*. Gama!" Omar mimed a scissors slicing a cable.

"So, old baldy cut you off."

This obviously could not be let go. It was like a personal challenge.

"Rambo," said Omar.

Benny nodded. "*First Blood*. This time it's personal."

They understood each other perfectly.

Sunday night was bed-early night. Benny nearly blew his hand by being too eager.

"I'm off so," he announced at nine fifteen.

"You can stay up to watch the end of the tractor pulling, if you like," said Pat Shaw.

"Tractor pulling!" scowled Benny. "Sure, that's not a sport at all."

"Well, whatever you like."

The Shaw parents had never been known to argue when Benny absented himself legally. Still, they couldn't help being a bit suspicious.

"So you're just going to bed, then, honey?"

"That's what I'm after saying, isn't it?"

"There's no need for that tone, Bernard. Take a shower before you pop off, would you?" Jessica got up from the stomach-bug couch. She had her Florence Nightingale face on. She smothered Benny in a pink mohair hug. "Thanks, Bernard," she said.

"For what, Ma . . . Mam?"

"Oh . . . I don't know. Everything. You've been so good this weekend. Not persecuting your brother. Staying out of trouble."

Benny felt like snail slime.

"You know, for a few days there we didn't think you were going to settle at all."

Pat Shaw waved a can of Celtia, the local beer, in Benny's direction. "Another week like this, and I'd say there's an excellent chance of your pocket money coming back online."

It was a cute move. The parents knew that this week was crisis time. God knows what missing the All-Ireland Final would make Benny do. Pocket money was the ultimate carrot. He hadn't had that since a little window-breaking episode last summer. It meant that he was risking a lot more than his health if he ventured out tonight. He was risking actual cash!

Georgie probably would have fallen to his knees, thanks gushing from his crawly mouth. But George was George, and Benny was Benny. He sort of grunted and shuffled off to the bathroom. There was zero hope that he could let Omar down. The little guy was relying on him.

Ma and Da didn't go to bed for ages. You'd swear it was for a bet. Some people would watch any old rubbish on the box. But eventually they popped off. Ma was the usual half hour scraping off her face and Da was well conked out before she even got to bed. Benny gave himself ten minutes' grace before hopping out the window.

The village was well lit up. Big fluorescent spheres floated on thin aluminium stalks. His partner was waiting behind the barrels.

"Welcome to part two," Omar whispered. Benny could only see eyes and teeth because Omar had covered his face with some kind of black gunge.

The little Tunisian was loaded down like a navy seal. Several lengths of co-ax cable were looped around his torso. Benny definitely wasn't going to ask where he'd got that from. He had a baseball cap on. Black, naturally. Around his waist hung a homemade Batman belt with various tools stuck into it. Finally there was an orange Stanley knife, tied around his neck with a piece of string.

"Holy God, Omar. It's not *Mission Impossible*."

Merrily whistling the theme, Omar began rubbing something squelchy into Benny's face. Benny, having had plenty of football boots in the gob in his day, knew immediately what it was.

"Shoe polish!" he spluttered. "Will you get off me, will ye?"

"Binny, eejit."

"I'll give ye eejit," said Benny, trying to scrape his tongue off with his teeth.

Omar pointed at Benny's face. "Ah . . . Omar, Binny . . . Bee Gees."

"Wha?"

"Bee Gees. Omar, Binny, Bee Gees."

"You mean we're like brothers with this gunk all over us?"

"Brothers, Binny?"

"Yes . . . *Na'am*. Bee Gees. Brothers."

This established, Omar was all business. He clamped his lips over dead giveaway white teeth and narrowed his eyes to slits. Thus disguised, he scuttled off into the village. Benny trailed behind. They made for the radio room, keeping in the shadows beneath the olive trees. There were maybe eight guards on duty, but nobody was expecting trouble. And even if they had been, the chances of any bunch of adults spotting a pair of boys with Benny and Omar's level of sneakiness was virtually nil. Except for maybe Mohamed Gama. And guess where he was? Planted smack bang outside the radio room. Right under the satellite dishes. He'd a big vigilant look on him too. If a horde of fundamentalists came swarming over that wall, Benny's few bob would've been on Mohamed.

"He's big," he breathed.

"Heavyweight champion," said Omar. "Undisputed."

Even in this light it was easy to imagine what sort of damage those wicked looking boots would do to your backside.

"Captain Sisco," said Omar, nodding at the guard.

"Michael Jordan," agreed Benny. Crouching here, watching this big lump of baldy aggression, Benny realized that maybe he didn't need another enemy just at the moment.

"Game over?" he said hopefully.

Omar was aghast. "The End? *Mafi* the end. Switch to plan B."

"Plan B?"

"*Na'am*. Binny plan."

"My plan. I don't have a plan."

"*Na'am*. Binny plan. B and E."

Beneath the polish, Benny reddened. B and E. Breaking and entering. His plan.

"*Mafi* B and E, Omar. Much bad juju."

That juju comment was a bit over the top, but Omar didn't even hear it. He was haring off around the back of the school. In seconds, he was over the fence like a greyhound and dodging through the monkey bars. Benny took off in pursuit. By the time he caught up, the Tunisian was squatting outside one of the bachelor units. At least back here, in the shadow of the village wall, they were concealed from the eyes and murderous intentions of Mohamed Gama.

"Plan B?" panted Benny.

"*Na'am*." Omar gave him a series of military hand signals.

"Righto, Arnold," snorted Benny.

Omar scuttled into the yard.

"What are you at, Omar, boy? Do you know what my da'll do to me if we're caught at this?"

Omar ignored him, wrestling a yellow gas cylinder from the concrete box. Benny just had to help him. The little chap would only drop it on his own. They rolled the bulky cylinder aside. Benny gave it a shake. Empty. At least they wouldn't actually die from an explosion. He turned around again and Omar was gone.

"Omar," he hissed. "C'mere, you little blackguard." Where was that fella? He heard a shuffling in the gas box and realized that Omar had actually managed to squeeze himself in there. Then he saw the hole, a foot-square gap in the hardwall or whatever. That little madman was in the house.

Trying to ignore an image of a fat, hairy, offshore worker with reinforced boots, Benny followed. Omar was unrolling his cable in the kitchen.

"*Kif halek*, Binny?"

"Shhh will ye, someone lives here."

"*Mafi* shh! Ghost town. Surprise, surprise, surprise, there's nobody home!"

Benny fervently hoped that for once Omar's English was accurate. He sneaked a peek into the sitting room. Not a stick of furniture. This unit wasn't occupied. He sighed. Well, thank God for that much, anyway.

Omar was hacking away at one end of his co-ax with an old pliers. In the corner of the sitting room a cable snaked up out of the concrete. Omar spliced it to his own. "I love it when a plan comes together," he announced grandly.

"Oh you're fluent, all right," scoffed Benny. "Sure, you've no clue what you're on about."

Omar produced a roll of electrical tape from the utility belt and put about twenty winds on the join. *"No problemo,"* he grunted, testing his handiwork. So now they had a link to the main antenna. If they could just get it back over the wall without a hiding, their mission would be complete.

The problem was how to run a length of quarter-inch cable through a house, across ten feet of grass, and over a wall without being busted by a psychopathic guard. The first part was easy. Benny knelt at the carpet edge and rolled it back. There was no underlay and the glue was patchy at best. Omar copped on quickly, tucking the co-ax under the lip of the carpet. That got them to the kitchen door.

The little Tunisian then produced another tool from his belt. A kitchen knife with the point worn off. With this he loosened a wall socket and slid it across a notch. There was a hole in the plaster. Bingo. They were in the kitchen.

Cupboards ran around the walls with pipe spaces at the back. It was too easy. Nothing would do Omar except to leap into the crawl space and run it along himself. Then it was just a matter of following the gas line back outside. Benny couldn't even remember why he was worried in the first place. Sure, they weren't even doing anything wrong! The worst he could be accused of was helping a disadvantaged African boy to share the wealth of First World countries. Da would go for that. 'Course he would.

They wriggled back out through the hole, careful to leave everything the way they'd found it. They rolled the cable to the end of the path, wedging the cord deep between the stone and clay. Even a lawnmower wouldn't get it down there. Benny went along behind, kicking the sod back in. That was a job he was well used to, having destroyed the front lawn several times himself with wild hurley swings.

The path branched off at a right angle, running parallel to the bachelor units. Their best bet from here was straight to the wall. As luck would have it, the rear loading gates were almost directly across from them. Cackling triumphantly, Omar plowed a path with his heel. Benny was on clean-up duty again. Stamp, stamp, cover.

The loading gate hadn't been opened for ages. Fancy looking Arabic writing that had once been white was now fungus spotted and bubbled with rust. They could go under handy enough, but if anyone ever actually opened the gate, the cable would be history. There were a few chunks of cracked cement along the frame where the wall wasn't quite flush. Benny picked one out and, lo and behold, it was only a cover-up job. There was a little tunnel clear to the other side. Eagerly they threaded the cable through. Too easy.

Benny was already mentally celebrating the switching-on ceremony. They had beaten that big baldy guard, and he didn't know a thing about it.

Luckily for them, they were away from the gate before it happened. A bit closer and Gama would surely have copped on to what they were at. As it was, the boys were halfway around the squash courts before they were spotted. The fact that Omar had fired up a cigarette and they were chuckling away might have had something to do with it.

They heard a roar that would shake a bull, and big-booted feet started bursting across the gravel toward them.

"Allah, Allah!" squeaked Omar, actually dropping his cigarette. He set off at a fierce pace, not even bothering to confirm who was after them. Benny did. He spared a second for a quick glance and then wished he hadn't. It was Gama. You couldn't see the face, just the silhouette of a huge frame and a single glint of moonlight bouncing off his bald head.

"Ya'lla, Binny!"

Without another second's hesitation, Benny *ya'lla*'ed. Gama was closing in, and his screaming had woken up the guard inside the courts—he hopped out the door with the look of someone who had been enjoying a sly nap not ten seconds previously. The building site was cut off. The fugitives veered off to the left, kicking up dust and gravel behind them. Benny giggled, waving at Omar as he went past.

"*Ya'lla*, yourself," he panted. This wasn't really a question of getting caught. There weren't a whole lot of adults around that could catch two young lads. The problem was running out of places to go. If they did have to go over the wall, the hard bit might be getting back in again.

Da would love that. The very evening they're telling him what a great son they have, he's out vandalizing, and fraternizing with the natives. He was sure that Gama couldn't have recognized them just yet. He was chasing their behinds, and both of them were keeping out of the light.

Benny was right about the pace, too. The guard was falling behind, sucking down strangled lungfuls of air. Great, thought Benny, until he noticed that Omar wasn't at his shoulder anymore. He glanced back. The poor chap was nearly done in. He was running hunched over, only his forward motion keeping his nose off the tarmac. Benny circled around to pick him up. Gama had stopped altogether at this stage. Benny opened his mouth for a taunt but stopped when he saw the guard spitting instructions into his walkie-talkie. In seconds there'd be blue suited hunter-seekers coming up out of the drains.

"Come on, tarry lungs," he said. "Get a move on."

To emphasize the urgency, he gave Omar a rousing

kick in the backside. That seemed to work. The Tunisian picked up pace and even seemed to have the energy left to mutter to himself.

There were roars coming from all quarters now. Walkie-talkie crackles mingled with the cricket chirps. Benny knew they only had one option, but he'd been trying to avoid it. He nudged Omar off the path. They leaned shoulder to shoulder and sped down through the family units. In seconds they were in front of an open window. Benny's bedroom.

"In you go, Omar boy." Omar didn't get the idea, but he copped on quick enough when Benny grabbed him by the utility belt and levered him through. Benny followed, making slightly less noise than a wounded elephant.

He was on his feet in a second, scrabbling at the window. First, the screen had to come down, then the window across, then the lace curtain. And with the net still swinging, Gama was there. Standing with his head cocked. Straining for some sign of the boys. Omar and Benny froze, not daring to duck down in case the movement would attract his attention. You never knew with this chap. Maybe he had one of those special connections with his surroundings the way hunters do. Maybe Gama could pierce sunshade and lace curtains with his hunter's vision. And for a second he did look at them, glaring, it seemed, right into their eyes. Then he was gone, scurrying into the darkness. The boys remembered to breathe.

"*Walahi,*" whispered Omar.

"*Walahi* is right. Now let's get you out before the goon squad comes back."

They crept into the corridor, but fate was conspiring against them. Jessica Shaw, woken by all the hubbub, gave her hubby a dig in the ribs. He rolled out of bed, trying to focus behind half closed eyelids, and made for the bedroom door.

Benny saw the handle turning. One shove, and before Omar knew what was going on, his nose was scraping the pink ducky bathmat. Benny locked the bathroom door behind them.

"Benny," said Pat. "That you in there?"

Benny looked at Omar. But he was getting no help from that quarter. Your man was too busy rubbing his grazed conk.

"Yeah, Da. It's me, all right."

"Well, what are you at? Strangling a hippo?"

Benny had to act fast. "I'm . . . Ah . . . having a shower"—of course, then he had to turn the water on. Pity about poor Omar in the bath.

"Allah!" he yelped.

"What are you saying?"

"Ah . . . I'll . . . ah . . . be finished in a minute."

"Didn't you have a shower already tonight?"

Benny groaned. He had. Of course he had. "Yeah . . . I did . . . But I got a bit sweaty . . ."

There was a short pause.

"Okay, son. Fair enough. Why don't you let me in? Maybe I could give you a hand."

So that's the way it was. Da didn't believe him. But he couldn't just come out and say that, so the two of them would have to talk around it.

"No . . . no, I'm grand, Da. I'm just drying off now."

"Sure, open up anyway. Your Mam will want to know what sort of mess you're after making."

"But I've no clothes on."

"Sure that's nothing I haven't seen a million times."

Think fast, boy. Your pocket money depends on it. "Actually, Da . . . I've wanted to chat about that sort of thing."

"What?"

"Well, I'm getting a bit old for all that. I'm not a baby, you know."

"Oh."

Aha. That got him.

"It's just, you know, I'm growing up, you know."

"I see. Of course." It was a clever move. Every parent's nightmare. Puberty. "Well, I'll leave you to it then. You're well able to look after yourself."

"Thanks, Da."

"G'night, Benny."

"'Night."

Safe. Benny felt a bit guilty playing on his da's awkwardness, but it was an emergency.

Omar was shivering in the bath, skin-colored patches appearing beneath the polish.

"Look at the state of you!" grinned Benny, twisting the mixer tap over to hot. "Might as well get all that gunge off you."

Ten minutes and several soapy protests later, Omar was standing by the back door with his clothes in a bag. He had one of Benny's old strips on him, and very nice it looked too.

"Up Wexford!" said Benny.

"*Na'am*. Up Wixfoord."

Benny cracked open the door and took a peek. Not a blue jumpsuited chap in sight.

"Righto, Omar, boy. Off you hop."

Blank stare.

"Ah . . . The End. That's all, folks."

Omar got it. "Ah . . . 'Night, John Boy."

"'Night, Grandaddy."

Omar grabbed Benny's hand and shook it, sort of formally, like you'd see old fellows do after the pub.

"Binny," he said seriously, "*shokran*."

"You're welcome. Now you'd better head away home."

Omar raised his hand, fingers split in a "V". "Live long and prosper," he said.

Benny closed the door and snuck back into bed.

8

FIT TO BE TIED

It was not a good week for Benny. Once the initial glow from the midnight cable affair had faded, he started thinking about the All-Ireland. There wasn't a single soul on the continent who understood what he was going through. Except perhaps his da, and, sure, you wouldn't see hide nor hair of him since he started that job. Benny was inconsolable.

As if things weren't bad enough, Harmony Rossi decided to take them on a field trip. In Benny's experience, there were two kinds of school tour. There were the educational types where some idealistic young one straight out of college thought the children wanted to learn on their day out. These usually involved a visit to the zoo, an interpretive center or, horror of horrors, somewhere like the Burren. The second was the kind favored by more experienced educators. These were the "hand-em-over" type. You go somewhere like Shielbaggin Outdoor

Education Center and let trained instructors wear the little darlings out.

Harmony had introduced a third category. It was the "abject poverty" tour. She pretended it was just an information tour, to see how Tunisia was developing its health care system, but Benny knew the idea was to expose these chubby, middle-class kiddies to the less privileged side of life. They would realize how well off they were and stop whining forever. So here they all were in the back of a Coaster bus on the way to some place that was actually called the Psychotic Farm, a hospital for handicapped children.

After a sweaty half hour on the bus, Harmony knocked on the big wooden gate. The door opened a crack and a smiling face appeared. The man spoke rapidly in French to Harmony. He turned out to be the school director, and a pretty cool sort of chap he was, too. He'd dark oily hair all brushed back, and a long, Al Pacino-type leather coat. He introduced himself as Samir Asaad and did the round of formal hand shaking. Samir had gone to college in Edinburgh and had decent English. It was funny, all the same, to hear a Scottish accent in this place.

"Good mornin', boys and gerruls," he said. To listen to him you'd swear he was going to beam up the lot of them.

Grace giggled—she couldn't help it—and was instantly mortified.

Samir grinned. "Och, I know. You weren't expecting that, were ye?"

"No," replied Grace. "I certainly wasn't."

"A Scot, is it? Rangers or Celtic?"

"Celtic."

Samir shrugged. "Ah well. No one's perfect."

And without their even realizing it, the class became relaxed. This chap is an expert, thought Benny.

"I'll give yez some background. We have here one of the few facilities of its kind in Tunisia."

There was a bit of a farmyard with a few outbuildings. Flaking paint revealed the same mud walls that ringed the school. Animals were roaming all over the place, as happy as Larry. Horses, turkeys, goats, and chickens trotted around affably, tasting anything that looked at all edible. As well as that there were about two dozen teenagers chasing around.

They went on the tour. First stop was the stable.

"This is where we keep the horses."

"Go on, is it?" Benny couldn't resist the opportunity.

Samir nodded at him. "Scottish?"

"Irish."

"I see," Samir smiled. It was not a happy smile. A gold tooth winked at the corner of his mouth. Benny recognized the look he was getting. It was a dare. Do that again and see what happens to you. Benny was on home territory.

"Every horse has two kids looking after it. They're responsible for that animal. You'd be amazed the effect looking after an animal has on these children—and on the animals."

It was true. The animals all looked in excellent condition. Shiny coats and no visible ribs. The Tunisian kids brushed the horses with heavy hands, talking to them all the time. Some just hugged them and cried. You couldn't help being moved.

"Each helper has four students to supervise. We also try to teach the children survival basics. Simple everyday procedures—toilet training, traffic safety, that sort of thing."

Even Benny knew not to make a smart remark there.

"Four is too many. One to one would be better. But we're lucky to have this facility at all."

One big hefty chap was in with the sheep. He seemed to be fighting them. He was on his knees in the mud, facing off a huge ram. A couple of women were trying to talk him out of the pen but he wasn't having any of it. The sheep made its move, head down, curved horns ready for business.

Curling stumpy fingers into a clublike fist, the boy hammered the unfortunate sheep right between the eyes. It was a sweet shot, threaded through the horns. The animal backed up a few steps, sneezed, and fell over. The Europeans were speechless.

"That's Wali," said Samir. "He gets a bit excited."

The two women had Wali by the elbows, trying to coax him away. They might as well have been flies for all the attention he was paying.

Samir strolled over to the pen. "Ya, Wali!"

Wali bolted upright, shedding his minders like dolls. His eyes cleared. "Samir," he hooted.

When someone roared at you like that, you could be fairly sure you were about to get your ribs crushed, one way or the other.

Wali tumbled over the fence and wrapped Samir in a bear hug. It was a close thing, but the director stayed upright. Wali must eat like a horse because he was absolutely massive. He was so big it was like joke fat.

"Say hello to Wali," grunted the director, smiling fondly at his gap-toothed captor.

Grace, being the big softy that she was, made the mistake of speaking. "Hello, Wali," she said, and you wouldn't have guessed that her smile was forced.

The big guy suddenly noticed that there were newcomers present. His expression changed, from grin to curiosity. He shrugged off Samir and lumbered toward Grace. Now you would know that her smile was forced. Harmony moved to intercept, but she bounced off him like a forward running into a fullback. It was the hair. Grace had blond hair. Wali moved in for a sniff. He gently lifted a handful from her neck and rubbed it under his nose.

A terrified squeak leaked between Grace's teeth like air from a balloon. It was Benny who saved her. He remembered trying to keep Georgie away from the fire guard when he was a toddler: you had to distract him. He dug out a box of Tic Tacs from his pocket and shook them beside the giant's ear. The effect was instantaneous. Wali's attention switched to the tantalizing rattle in his ear.

It was part two of the plan that went a bit astray. Benny was visualizing himself lulling the giant to sleep, then kindly placing the Tic Tacs in his pocket. Of course, then he'd get a few hero hugs and a bit of adulation.

This was the plan. What happened was a tad different. With the same swiftness he'd demonstrated with the sheep punching, Wali wrapped five massive digits around the box of mints. Only Benny's proficiency at whipping his hand out of the path of hurleys more or less saved his fingers. But it didn't save the Tic Tac box.

Benny blew on his semi-crushed fingers. Well, at least Grace was free. But Wali wasn't finished yet. His grab brought him lurching forward, bumping Benny off both feet. Benny sailed backward for a couple of yards, then landed on a turkey. Yes, a turkey. Just his luck.

Wali began the delicate task of picking mints from the shattered plastic, while his victim writhed in the dust trying to suck air into his chest.

"Oh the poor turkey," said Zoe. They pulled Benny up to see if the bird was all right.

"Sorry about that, pal," said Samir, not looking at all sorry. "Now we will continue our tour."

There was a paddock out the back. A young lad was racing around on the back of a shiny brown horse. Benny recognized a poseur when he saw one. Your man would gallop right up to the corner and then viciously haul the poor horse's head around. There was no need for that sort of thing. He was just showing off for the visitors. Of course the girls squealed away dutifully. Benny was disgusted. Women were impressed by anything.

"Gianni is from Italy," said Samir. "He is our horse rider. Anyone that has the coordination to ride, he's the laddie that teaches them."

Your man Gianni was Italian, all right. He'd tight jodhpurs and a big flouncy white shirt on him. He must have thought he was a pirate or something. Gianni yanked the horse to an abrupt halt in front of the eighth graders. You could nearly hear the girls' hearts beating faster.

"Ciao," he said.

"Chow," said Benny.

Gianni ignored him. "Maybe de *bella donna* would like on de horse a sit?"

The *bella donna* nodded like their chins were on springs.

Harmony wasn't so sure. She was, after all, American,

and her first thought was: lawsuits. "I don't know," she said. "That sure is a big animal."

"Ees a perfectly save," said Gianni, sort of oozing off the horse. "I holda de reins, you taka de photo."

"Oh please, Harmony. He's so, like, cool—the horse, I mean."

"Go on, then. Tell him no riding, Samir. Just sit and photo, that's it."

"I understand dere not to be de riding," said Gianni.

So they all hopped up, one after the other. Harmony fidgeted through the whole thing, snapping photos without even pointing the lens. Benny rolled his eyes. Sure, what could go wrong? It was like sitting on a fence.

Gianni pointed at him. "*Tu*. Now you."

Benny paled. That fence-horse comparison was starting to seem a bit weak.

"Go on, Benny," said Grace. It was the first time she'd talked to him all week.

"Grand," said Benny, putting on his downtown strut. "No bother at all."

He ducked in through the fence and gave the horse an eyeballing. *I am the master*, he broadcast. *You must obey*. The horse snorted. *Come on, sucker*, he beamed back. *Just put your foot in the stirrup*. Benny made a mental note to have words with whoever had told him that story about staring down animals.

Now to get up. It'd be nice to make it without that Italian smoothy's help. If only that stirrup yoke wasn't at eye level. He took a swing at it. He would've made it too, no bother, but Gianni decided to lend a hand anyway. He grabbed Benny by the backside and gave him a mighty hooch. Benny plopped down on the saddle, an expression of strangled indignation on his face. Harmony, naturally, chose that moment to snap a photo. This was also the moment that Wali decided to finish the Tic Tacs. He also decided that he wanted more.

Benny regained his composure, for about half a second. Then he noticed the big lad coming over the fence. The horse noticed it, too. It was one of those slow-motion sort of things. The class did a collective "Oh!" with their gobs. Samir's cigarette slipped right out from between his lips. Benny could feel his mount's back muscles bunching through the saddle. But the worst thing of all was that Gianni, the ice-cool Mister Slippery Suave, dropped the reins. Now there was nothing controlling the beast.

Benny tried broadcasting again. *Be calm, horsey. Calm. I am the master.* The horse knew he was lying. And with Wali mere centimeters away, it decided to jettison excess baggage. One buck was more than enough. A ripple ran from the animal's ears to his tailbone. And Benny was airborne. First the turkey, now this. How long could a streak of bad luck last?

He noticed a few things while he was up there. Funny how your brain picked out details. Probably trying to distract you from impending death. He saw that everyone was watching the horse, except Grace. That Harmony's roots were gray. Hah! There went her credibility! No hippie worth her tie-dye would disguise something as natural as gray hair. Also, from this altitude he noticed another building over behind the stables. White walls and barred windows. There was one more thing. Down in the corner of a grimy window. It was a hand. A little brown hand rubbing streaks in the glass.

Then Benny hit the apex of his curve and started on the descent. Nothing below but hard ground. There was never a turkey around when you needed one. Something was definitely going to get broken. Benny closed his eyes. But the big impact never came. Instead he was cushioned by what felt like a sofa, complete with padded arms. It was Wali. The big lad just snatched him out of the air. But only because he wanted to search for more mints. Samir swapped Benny for a hard sweet.

"Thanks," panted Benny.

"Nae problem, laddie," grinned Samir, gold tooth glinting.

Harmony gathered them all hurriedly. "I think that's enough excitement for one day," she announced. She was badly shaken, having just lived through a million-dollar negligence suit in the past few moments. She had made a decision: this visit was going to be over before anyone was seriously damaged. Nobody moaned or groaned. Her point was made, anyway: everyone realized how lucky they were, and now they just wanted to go home.

Benny lagged behind. "Hey, Samir," he called, lurching over to the director.

"Yes . . . ah . . ."

"Benny."

"Yes, Benny?"

"That white building over there. What's in that, anyway?"

Samir's face lost that look of polite interest that you switch on for visitors. "Ah . . . nothing. Nothing that you want to see."

Benny thought about arguing, but bad things happen in threes. And after the turkey and the horse, he might be better off keeping his trap shut.

Here it was at last: All-Ireland Sunday, and Benny and his da were plonked on the couch watching sumo wrestling on Eurosport. As if that wasn't bad enough, the international phone lines were down so they couldn't even get someone to give them a buzz with the score. Benny asked about faxing and Da gave him a look reserved for the terminally dopey. Of course the Doctor Spock–reading parent in him regretted this, and he explained that fax also operated on phone lines.

So the pair of them sat glaring at the TV set. Jessica squeezed between them.

"So how are my two men?"

No reply.

"Anyone for tea or a Coke?"

"No. No thanks, honey."

She put her arm around each of them. "Come on now, boys. We can have fun without some silly ball game, can't we?"

Pat Shaw got a bit snappy, which was unusual for him. "Jessie, this is not *Mary Poppins* and you're not Julie Andrews."

Benny winced.

"Fine. You two just sit there and mope. Georgie and I will get on with our lives."

So off they went to the pool, leaving Benny and Da to stew in their own depression. And stew they did, squirming around on the sofa until hunger drove them to the kitchen. Three o'clock came. They'd be squaring up for the puck-off now. Croke Park would be alive with roaring and singing, with swaying banners and supporters of all ages. You wouldn't be able to move through the streets of Dublin on anything bigger than a scooter. It was funny how depression could bond people together. Pat and

Benny developed a deep and abiding hatred for the rest of the world. It was everybody's fault. EuroGas for shipping them. Tunisia for having natural resources. Sky Sports for not broadcasting this far south.

Five o'clock. The match was over. The bonfires would be lighting now. Da kept checking the phone. Every ten minutes he'd punch in the international code and then whack down the receiver when he got the Arabic message.

"Stupid television," said Benny.

"Yeah."

"You wait your whole life."

"I know."

"Every year they lose the Leinster. Every year."

"Like clockwork."

"Except this year, of course."

"You'd think it was for a bet."

Dinner was pretty grim. Benny hacked some fish fingers into a million pieces and then sloped off to bed. All this misery, and school tomorrow, too. Youth was hell. He drifted off into a colorful sleep. The purple and gold of Wexford were the colors.

A knock on the window woke him up. For a second he lay there, trying to remember what roused him from his blubbery dream. Another series of raps shook the chalet. This was no gentle lobbing of gravel. Someone was whacking the screen with the heel of their hand. Benny clattered over to the curtains. Omar's grin was shining in at him through the darkness.

"What is it?" he hissed, throwing open the window. Omar vaulted into the room, bowling Benny back onto the bed. At another time this might have been a bit of a laugh, but not on the most miserable night of Benny's young life. Eventually he subdued the bony Tunisian, pinning him with the classic knees-on-shoulders position.

"Cop on, Omar," said Benny, keeping the decibels down with heroic effort. "You're going to get me corpzublicked."

"Corp-zoo-blicked?"

"Dead. Bang-bang. Hung from the neck."

Omar's grin didn't falter, not for a second. He simply rattled a little black package under Benny's nose and mispronounced one word.

"Skee," he said, eyebrows raised, waiting for Benny to get it.

"Ski? What ski? Omar, you are really starting to . . ." Benny got it. It had taken a few seconds, but it was late and he wasn't as sharp as usual. "Skee?" he spluttered. "Sky! You mean Sky Three?"

"Duh," said Omar.

The package was a video. Benny grabbed it with trembling fingers. "No . . . you're having me on."

"Skee tree," nodded Omar, and then taking advantage

of Benny's lapse in concentration, he dumped his friend onto the floor. Benny rolled in midair to protect the video. He was up in a heartbeat.

"How, Omar?"

"Omar okay."

"No, eejit! How did you do this? I don't understand."

"Pass."

"Video . . ."

"*Na'am.*"

"Where . . . ah . . . *ou?*" Bit of bilingualism there.

"Ah . . . *ou.*" Omar understood all right, he was just dragging out the agony.

"Omar!"

"Aiwa! Omar and Ali. Murtaugh and Riggs. Ali Chekov EuroGas."

Benny concentrated. This was a long burst of TV lingo. "Right, so your buddy Ali drives for EG."

"*Na'am.* Ali Homer Tunis. Homer Skee Tree. Ali Dulles International *Die Hard,* Homer Ali All Eye-er-land."

That one was a bit harder.

"Let's see . . . Ali's da lives in Tunis. He's got Sky and he gave your buddy the tape on an EG run to the airport." It made sense. It could even be true.

There were times in your life when you couldn't worry about consequences. You had to rely on your da to ignore the breaching of several domestic taboos. With the sacred video clutched to his heaving chest, Benny burst into the parents' room.

"Da! I've got it. The final! On video!"

Pat Shaw's brain had a few layers of Celtia to swim through before it reached consciousness, but Jessica shot up immediately.

"Benny, what?"

Then, of course, she saw Omar and thought they were being invaded. And even if they weren't, someone had seen her without makeup. "Get out!" she shrieked, disappearing behind a sheet tent.

Pat opened his eyes. "Hmm?"

"Da, listen to me," said Benny urgently. He had the feeling that if they didn't watch this soon, it would disappear like one of Cinderella's props. "I have a tape of the match. I'm going to watch it now. Okay?"

"Good man, Benny," muttered his da, burrowing down into the pillow. "You fire ahead."

Benny realized that this was about as close as he was going to get to actual permission. He gave his da one more shake and then scooted off down to the sitting room. Omar bobbed along behind him, thoroughly enjoying his friend's excitement.

Benny dived at the video recorder, arms outstretched, the rough carpet burning his knees. Michael Lester's chirpy voice came out of the speakers before they even got pictures. It used to really annoy Benny that Lester was so happy all the time, especially as it usually coincided with Benny himself being miserable, but now the commentator's voice seemed to stand for everything he'd left behind. It took ages for the pictures to focus, but by the time the figures went from fuzzy jelly-bean shapes to the crisp, flashing jerseys of the Wexford team, Pat Shaw was shouldering himself along the wall.

"Ah . . . Son . . . What did you say you had?"

"Quiet, Da, it's starting."

With a gurgling sound, Pat stretched himself on the floor beside his boy.

"Quiet!" he roared at no one in particular. Eventually, after a few ads for fertilizer and Guinness (the PR boys really knew their audience), the ball was thrown in.

The crowds were going mad right from the word go. You'd know from the noise of them that they'd been waiting for nearly twenty years for this moment. You don't get this frantic in twelve months. It takes a generation to build up.

The team list flashed up on the screen. Benny searched it eagerly. George O'Connor was in! Flood must have an injury or something. Unfortunately Owen O'Neill was in for Limerick too. The ankle must be better.

Benny and Da sang along with the national anthem.

The Wexford supporters started roaring halfway through, unable to contain themselves any longer.

Benny felt sick. After all this time his dream was being played out on the field before him. Tough and even, neither side giving an inch without a fight. It was almost impossible to watch. There were only minutes left. Wexford were ahead, but there was still time for Limerick to snatch a victory. Limerick bulled through into the Wexford box. The sliotar went everywhere except in the goal. The Shaws groaned like men on the rack. Even the crowd was hoarse. The cheers were raw now, like a seashell roaring in your ear. They were into extra time. Two minutes.

"Blow it up!" squealed Benny. So close, yet one shot could change it. "Blow it up!"

The ref must have heard him. Because he blew the whistle. Game over.

To the Shaws it was almost beyond belief. After so long waiting for it to happen, it was hard to realize that Wexford were champions at last. The crowd invaded the pitch, mobbing the players.

Da grabbed Benny and swung him around by the armpits. When they were finished hugging and crying, Pat decided he had to tell Jessica. She, of course, was on the armchair behind him, where she'd been for the previous ninety minutes.

"Did you see . . . ?"

"Yes, honey."

"I never thought . . ."

"I know, honey."

"It was just no bother to them at all . . ."

"No, honey."

Funny the way hurling robs you of the ability to form sentences.

"Pat?"

"Yes?"

"Who's that?"

Omar sat cross-legged on the sofa, chewing away on some leftover fish fingers.

"I . . . ah . . . it's . . . Who is that, Benny?"

When you'd forgotten your homework as many times as Benny had, excuses came easy. "That's Omar. He's one of the guards' young lads. I've been teaching him to play hurling." Not bad. But there were a few holes.

"What's he doing up at this hour?"

"His da is on night shift."

"And?"

Benny used one of his favorite tricks. Admit a minor sin to hide a major one. "Come on, Mam. He snuck out of the hut to give me the tape. One of the drivers brought it down from Tunis."

"Well, maybe Omar would like something to drink with those fish fingers."

Bingo! They bought it. Well, Jessica bought it. Da couldn't have cared less where the tape came from. If Jack the Ripper had passed it in with blood dripping from its spools, Pat Shaw would have thanked him and slapped it into the recorder.

"Coke?"

Omar shook his head. "*Laa. Mafi* Coke. Pepsi, the choice of a new generation!"

"Don't push your luck." Benny tried a scowl but couldn't pull it off. Wexford were the All-Ireland champions and he had lived to see it. "Pepsi it is, my good man," he said, dancing off into the kitchen.

Omar nodded under Jessica's scrutiny.

"So, how long have you known our Benny?"

"Binny. Binny eejit."

"I see," said Jessica. "You're quite the joker."

"Holy rusted metal, Batman."

"Really?"

"Binny, Omar. Bee Gees."

"Pardon?"

"Nobody gets too much love anymore," warbled Omar, eager to make a good impression on the parent, even if it was only the mother.

Benny skidded back into the room. "Omar," he said,

using the tone usually reserved for Mother Teresa or Neil Diamond, "I'm not going to forget this in a hurry."

Pat sniffed. "Thanks, Omar. You're a sound man."

They shook hands enthusiastically. This boy could do no wrong in the Shaw household tonight. He was almost as much a hero as the lads on the field.

Jessica had a few suspicions about this grubby little bearer of gifts, but for tonight at least he was beyond reproach. Just in case there was something underhanded going on, though, Jessica gave Omar that Kathleen Turner look that said: *I'm watching you, mister.*

Omar swallowed. Suddenly that Arab conviction about women being the weaker sex seemed a bit dodgy.

9

CORPZUBLICKED

Over the following weeks the two lads mooched around the general vicinity, not trying too hard to stay out of mischief. Da Shaw swallowed the old "son of a guard" story, so Omar was even welcome in the house. Then again, "welcome" might be a bit strong. Not actually ejected would be closer to the mark.

Whenever Benny reminisced about this period, he saw it as a time of great learning; two boys selflessly giving of their cultures so that both might become more cosmopolitan. Jessica, on the other hand, remembered them as two mucky hooligans who could scarcely look at a window without breaking it. Benny often thought that his parents were secretly pleased when he fouled up because it gave them a legitimate excuse to practice their sarcasm. So, in a way, whenever he misbehaved he was doing Ma and Da a favor.

In fact, Pat and Jessica Shaw were over the moon that

their son had a new crony. But it wouldn't do to let Benny see that or he might decide not to pal around with the little guard's son anymore. Rule five of the "almost a teenager" handbook: Whatever pleases your parents is, by definition, evil. So Jessica treated young Omar to the same dirty looks that any of Benny's old Wexford buddies got. This kept her son happy and it gave her a chance to practice her Juno face.

Of course, Omar wasn't always available. He had to go about the boring activity of keeping himself alive. Omar was a kind of Tunisian Arthur Daly. He would buy or sell anything that could earn him a profit. To the untrained eye, most of his merchandise resembled a heap of junk, but to Omar there was a market for almost anything. You just had to know where that market was. And the boy seemed to have a natural gift for that sort of thing.

The village was a treasure trove. The building site yielded blocks, timber, nails, screws, and steel rods. Those rods were a lot of work, though. You had to transport them by dragging them behind the moped. One to three inches could be lost off the length, depending on how far you had to drag the merchandise.

Day-to-day questions were answered, too. Omar didn't have a loo as such, or maybe it was fairer to say that he had hundreds of them scattered all over the place. He also used the vacant bachelor chalet, sneaking in for midnight baths or a quick blast of his gear in the washing machine. It was a weird sort of existence. But Omar seemed happy and healthy enough, whatever about clean.

The Shaws' shipment arrived, and with it Benny's spare hurley and hurling gear. He set about teaching Omar how to play, and in a month they were having reasonable puck-abouts in the olive grove. Benny enjoyed roaring abuse at his friend. He was of the Father Barty school of coaching, where nothing good ever came of encouragement. Fear of the consequences was the only way to make a young chap learn.

In spite of himself, Benny began to loosen up. He didn't even feel the need to be smart all the time, which is not to say that he didn't take advantage of an opportunity when it arose.

It was a wonder the two boys weren't killed a hundred times. Between haring around on the back of the moped and leaping off the top of the perimeter wall, they used up enough lives for a whole sackful of cats. It never occurred to Benny or Omar that their luck had to change sometime.

Benny showered voluntarily one Saturday night. Omar had asked him over for dinner at his shack. The little fellow was so serious about it that Benny reckoned he'd better give the old noggin a scrub. Ma and Da had gone off into town for a spot of grub with the Tafts. He'd easily be back before them. The Crawler could babysit himself. Benny smiled.

He caught sight of himself passing the mirror and grimaced. His eyes and teeth were looking awful white. Then he realized that they were grand, it was the rest of him that was brown. Declare to God, if he wasn't getting a tan! Finally he was starting to look a bit healthy. And it wasn't one of those lying-by-the-pool type tans, either. This was a deep brown windburn like you'd get on a fisherman's forearms. Benny stepped in closer to see if he could spot any more changes. He searched the top lip for some fluff—nothing. The hair was going mad altogether. Whatever the sun was doing to it, it was a lot stiffer now. Sticking out at right angles to his head. Benny spotted a few ginger strands among the brown. Ginger! And if anything, he had more scabs and bites than ever, but suntan, much like deodorant, hid a multitude.

The Crawler was on the sofa in his dressing gown. What other young lad on the planet would wear a dressing gown outside of a hospital ward? But Georgie boy had it on him at every opportunity. Parading around like some sort of little lord.

"How come you're washing yourself?" he asked suspiciously.

Benny automatically began to formulate an excuse and then remembered who he was talking to. "Shut up, you, or you'll get a dead arm for yourself. What's on the box?"

"*National Velvet* is on TNT." Georgie loved Elizabeth Taylor, especially the younger model.

"You'll be lucky." Benny grabbed the remote.

"Ah . . . Benny!"

Sure, who cared? He was going out anyway. "Go on, then. Anything for a quiet life. Don't say I never do anything for you."

George smiled delightedly. "Thanks, Benny," he said.

Benny hated when he did that. It made him feel guilty about slying out when he was supposed to be babysitting. But what could happen? There was a boy, a couch, and a TV. Not a dangerous element in the entire equation. If it was an equation.

With a final glare, Benny went off down to his room, leaving his brother in charge of the remote control. When you're the youngest in a family, this doesn't happen very often after five o'clock and is an event to be savored.

Benny dressed himself in the bedroom, trying to reason his way out of the nagging guilt. On the minus side: he was disobeying a direct order not to leave the unit. If rumbled, he could forfeit his recent reacquaintance with cash. He was also deserting his younger brother, leaving him at the mercy of rampaging mosquitoes or whatever.

However, his ma was always saying how Georgie was more mature than him anyway, so what was the point of leaving him in charge? None whatsoever. And this dinner thing was obviously important to Omar. He'd had a big serious head on him when he was asking. It wouldn't be right to disappoint his only buddy for selfish reasons, like trying to stay out of trouble. Now, Benny knew there were more holes in this reasoning than in an octopus's underpants, but he had a knack of picking whatever logic suited him at the time. So, guilt duly vanquished, he rolled up the mosquito screen and went out the window.

Omar was prodding a stick into a campfire when his European buddy arrived. He had a big fez on him, made out of red velvety stuff, with little bits of mirror stuck all over it. His trousers were the white, baggy, nappy-type ones that you'd see the old Bedouin bushboys wearing. But the jacket was the best bit. It was like a Communion one, only made of the same fluorescent blue material you'd see in cycling shorts. Benny reckoned that this was Omar's equivalent of "going to see Grandad on Christmas Eve" clothes. Obviously something was up.

"*Ya*, Omar," he said.

"*Ya*, Binny. *Kif halek?*"

"Sure, grand I suppose." He pointed at Omar's hat. "What's the story with that thing?"

Omar removed the sparkling hat reverentially and rubbed the shiny bits. "Hat." he said.

"Go on. Is it?"

"Hat Homer."

Benny thought for a second. Then he remembered. Homer was TV talk for Da. "It's *trés . . . trés . . .* nice," he said, reinforcing this with two thumbs up.

"Shokran."

"You're welcome."

Omar handed him the hat. He was that serious you'd swear he was Geronimo passing the peace pipe. Benny saw now that the velvet was indeed covered in little bits of mirror. Crusty knobs of glue leaked around the edges of the glass. Orange flames and his own uncertain face were bounced back at him.

"Tres nice," he said again, trying to pass back the old and slightly pongy heirloom, or hair-loom, he thought, swallowing a giggle, but no, Omar was having none of it.

"Negatory good buddy," he said. "On your head be it."

Benny knew the drill with these Arab types. If you didn't burp after a meal or if you refused their kindness, they were liable to get very annoyed and swear out a fatwah on you and your family.

"Right-ee-oo," he said, delicately balancing the fez on his ears. Instantly his imagination ran riot, flashing up images of crawly things abseiling onto his scalp.

Omar went back to poking the fire. He was in an awful somber mood tonight, thought Benny. Still, though, when you lived in a hut and your parents had died in a train crash or something, you were entitled to the odd off day.

Eventually the young Tunisian raked off the sticks and ash to reveal a mound of flat stones underneath. These were flipped away, hissing and splitting. Benny stared; he'd never seen rocks glow before. They seared little craters for themselves like mini flying saucers. Beneath this makeshift oven was a red clay pot. Like one of those Greek vases with handles. Omar hauled the pot out with his stick and dumped it on a sheet of newspaper.

"Gargoulette," he said proudly.

"Gargle it?"

"La," said Omar shaking his head. *"Gargoulette!"*

"Oh I get it," nodded Benny, the fez rocking on his ears. "That's a *gargoulette*."

Omar picked up a brick and handed it to Benny. Benny licked a finger and touched the stone. No hiss. It wasn't part of the oven then. "So?" he asked, hefting the rock.

Omar clapped his hands together. "So, blow it, Murdock."

No boy on the face of the planet could have resisted an offer like that. Benny drew back his fist and plunged the rock into the rounded belly of the *gargoulette*. The baked clay imploded, forcing out the contents. Thick greasy gravy, onions, and hot couscous splashed along his forearm.

"Great taste at McDonald's," laughed Omar.

"Kentucky Fried Chicken," agreed Benny, licking his arm. The cracked curves of the *gargoulette* were brimming with chunks of meat and couscous. The top was stoppered with a crusty, baked lump of dough. Omar grabbed an arc of broken pottery and dragged it through the guts of the feast.

"Al-hamdu li'llah," he said, waving the makeshift bowl vaguely toward Mecca. Grace over, he dropped a steaming lump of meat into his upturned gob. Benny followed the leader. This was how you were supposed to eat. Plenty of gnashing and grunting. No cutlery or anything that might slow you down. Just tear off whatever you wanted from the steaming mush and stuff it down your gullet.

The bread was wonderful, dipped in gravy but still crunchy. Benny forgot that he didn't like onions. He forgot that he always separated his food groups at home. He also forgot that he wasn't supposed to drink the local water. But he might get a reminder of that later. The whole job took less than ten minutes. Benny gave Omar the thumbs-up. He wasn't able to talk just yet, but he did remember his manners and summoned up the most resounding burp he could muster. Omar snorted disdainfully and let one rip that would have inflated several balloons. Benny applauded gently; you had to accept when you were out-classed.

They collapsed in the dirt, watching the night drop down. The stars were getting more confident now, twinkling away through the last streaks of blue. Benny started feeling a bit poetic.

"Do you see that little star?" he breathed. "I wish I could drive there in my car."

"*Vorsprung durch technic,*" burped Omar.

They lay there for ages, watching the sky, listening to the night sounds of Africa. The strays were out, howling away to beat the band. You could even hear the sound of car horns from Tyna spreading out over the desert like the cries of some weird animal. This is the life, thought Benny. You get one half-decent evening like this and it makes up for a lot.

Omar roused him with a poke. "*Ya*, Benny," he said, holding out a framed picture. Benny took a look. It was a group photograph. "The Waltons," said Omar.

Benny focused. At last something on the elusive family. There were four of them in it, posed real formally in front of one of those mottled photographer's backdrops.

"There's you, Omar. I nearly didn't recognize you without muck all over you."

Omar pointed with a grubby finger. "Homer . . . Bouya."

"That's your da. He's a big chap . . . Rambo."

"*Na'am. Shuf Ummee.*"

"What?"

"Ah . . . Marge."

"So that's Ma."

"*Na'am sahbee. Shuf Ukht,*" Omar sighed. "*Kaheena.*"

"That's your sister . . . *Ukht?*"

"*Na'am.* Kaheena."

"Kaheena?"

"*Na'am.*"

"Look at her. She's tiny. So, what's the story with her?"

"Pass."

"Ah . . . Omar. Kaheena Chicago Hope?"

"*Na'am.*"

"Upset stomach. Ask for Rennie?"

"*La.* Upset stomach, ask for Rennie." He tapped his forehead. "*Mokh. Mushkela.* Panadol gets to the pain fast." Omar rolled his eyes and waggled his tongue. Benny nearly laughed until he realized his friend wasn't trying to be funny.

Omar took the picture back and stroked the glass. A couple of fat tears blobbed down his nose. "Kaheena," he breathed, the word barely coming through his sadness. "Kaheena, Kaheena."

This was getting a bit serious. They were supposed to be having a Huck and Tom sort of time: two lads mucking around, maybe getting into the odd bit of mischief, none of your girly emotions.

"You all right there, Omar, boy? Ah . . . *Sh'nawalek?*"

Omar sniffed. *"Al-hamdu li'llah,"* he recited automatically.

But he wasn't all right. Not really. Benny was always at a loss in these sorts of situations. Bawling people always put him off his stride. Made him feel it was his fault somehow. He hooked an arm around the little chap's shoulder.

"Omar, Binny. Bee Gees!"

Omar nodded limply. *"Na'am.* Bee Gees."

But even the major thrill of having a European friend couldn't drag him out of his mope. This was real misery and sorrow. The kind Benny had never come up against before. It changed his friend completely. It snuffed out the light in his eyes, rounded his shoulders and tightened his muscles. How were you supposed to get over something like that? Benny's forehead prickled with shame at the memory of all the dopey hours he'd spent feeling hard done by. Suddenly having no pocket money didn't seem like a gi-normous deal.

Omar snorted mightily, his head going back with the force of it. Then after a quick gargle he spat on the fire. Steam rose like a frightened snake. He jumped up and shook himself, throwing off his depression.

"Binny," he said, still sounding a bit on the serious side.

"Yeah?"

"Binny, Omar. *Khouya*."

"Wha'?"

"Bee Gees. Binny, Omar."

"Righto. We're brothers. *Na'am*."

Omar smiled. He had decided something. "Jon—Ponch."

"We're going on the bike? Where . . . *Ou?*"

"*Feesa, sahbee*. Hurry up, friend."

"Yeah, yeah. Not Wembley Stadium though."

"*Mafi* Wembley," replied Omar, pedal-starting the ancient Peugeot. "Chicago Hope."

Benny scrambled to his feet, the fez bobbing down over his eyes. So they were going to drop in on Omar's sister. With barely a second's thought, he hopped on the moped. This was getting easier—sure, if you didn't get caught the first time, why would you get nabbed now?

They took off across the scrub, the bumpy terrain trying to knock a few disks out of their backbones. The spices in Benny's meal started coming back to haunt him. He had a cringy thought.

"Hey, Omar. Where's the other turkey?"

But Omar couldn't speak English, and anyway the bike was long gone before the words could catch up. Just as well.

* * *

The spin into town was as touch and go as ever. Diesel fumes and close shaves with death were the order of the day. Old chaps with raggy gums screeched Arabic abuse on the way past. Some took a swing with whatever cargo they happened to be holding. Benny nearly lost the fez after a blow with a stiff pink fish.

"*Beleed!*" howled Omar.

It was catchy, easy to remember and probably not a compliment. Still, though, if you didn't actually know it was a curse then it couldn't be a sin to use it.

"*Beleed!*" Benny shouted after the fish-wielder. "*Beleed! Beleed!*"

Judging by your man's rolling eyes and flapping jaws, the word had the right effect. The fisherman was so surprised to see a white face spouting Arabic that he hopped his front wheel off the curb. *Beleed.* One for the files.

Finally the jolting spin came to an end. Omar wheelied on to the verge, bouncing the back wheel after him. Benny stepped off gingerly. It was possible that he would never walk straight again. There was a wind trail of tears blasted from the corners of his eyes.

Omar lit a cigarette off one of the bike's pipes.

"I've been here before," Benny said, looking around him. They were at the Psychotic Farm.

"Chicago Hope," whispered Omar. "Kaheena."

"This is not a hospital, Omar."

Omar shrugged. It was close enough.

Benny plucked the cigarette from Omar's gob.

"Omar Chicago Hope," he said, crushing the butt like an annoying insect.

The Tunisian rolled his eyes. Yeah, yeah, yeah.

In truth, Benny was stalling. He didn't really want to pay a return visit to this place. The last time, he'd been flattened, dumped, and humiliated. And that was in broad daylight, with all the staff hanging around. Who knew what could happen at this time of night.

Omar tapped him on the shoulder. Ah well, so much for not going in. A moment later they were astride the clay wall.

"*Shuf*," said Omar, pointing at a low white building.

"I see it," said Benny. He remembered the hand behind the bars. Small bony fingers rubbing circles in the dirt.

Omar put a finger to his lips. "*Uskut.*"

Benny snorted. Like he had to be told.

They hopped down into the paddock. A fat horse flapped its lips at them. Omar flapped back. Having cleverly circumvented the security, they trotted to the target building. The walls were cool and damp. Furry mold slimed beneath their fingers. Omar ignored the first three windows, turning the corner to the blind side.

"Plan B," he grinned. "B and E."

Maybe Benny might have backed out then. He might

have said, *Hold the horses there, boyo, we're breaking into a school here after hours. We could end up in some African prison with no running water.* But he was far from home and Omar was going in anyway.

The window was at head height and lined with rusty bars.

Omar winked. *"Shuf."*

Benny looked. The bars pulled out of the clay like a wellie out of muck.

"You've been here before," he commented.

"Uskut!"

"Uskut, yourself. There's only the horses listening."

Omar laced his fingers. *"Feesa, sahbee."*

"I'm going. I'm going."

Benny was well versed in the art of the leg up. The time-honored tradition of orchard robbing requires a certain skill in scaling walls. The secret to a successful leg up was coordination. You had to pull and get boosted at the same time. Otherwise the liftee was only so much dead weight for the lifter.

Benny caught the ledge and hauled. Omar lifted. It was perfect. Nine-point-nine for the take off. Zero for the landing. He whacked his head on a concrete lintel and tumbled into the building like a bag of rubbish. He was lying on a bed or something, staring into the blackness. Then the sky fell on his head.

Some big, hairy backs had landed on Benny in his day, but never anything like this. Whatever it was just wrapped around him like a hairy duvet. Benny felt a tongue the size of a slipper rasping up his chin. He started kicking and squealing, but his assailant absorbed blows and sound with sheer bulk. Omar joined in the row, wedging a bony leg between Benny and the mystery attacker.

"*Ya*, Wali! Ismee, Omar!"

Wali! The name brought back big, woolly memories. The infant in a giant's body dropped Benny like a rat in a bag.

"Omar!" he roared. "Omar, Omar!" And carried him off up between two rows of cots. It was funny looking at them. Like some sort of strange animal with two spare legs sticking out of its belly.

Benny followed the shadowy bundle through the building. The place was a bit stinky. Like babies and old wardrobes. There were people on the beds. Kids, judging by the shapes. Most of them were making sleep sounds, but some followed him with dark eyes. Benny was getting really scared. There wasn't a sinner who knew where he was. He could die here and they'd never find him.

"Omar," he said, hearing a bit of a whine in his own voice. He sounded like Georgie. One more corner to go and he'd have them. Assuming that was a good thing. It was a bit like chasing after the hurricane that took your house.

His eyes were picking up details from the gray gloom. What he saw scared him even more. There were rings mounted in the walls, with chains running through them. Metal bedpans poked out from under the beds. Massive insects skittered across the concrete floors, the tapping of their sturdy feet dug into Benny's brain like ice-picks.

He caught up with Little and Large. They were hunkered at the end of the last bed. Omar had a scary look on his face. His eyes were wide and wild.

"Kaheena," he whispered.

There was a sleeping girl in the bed. Benny tiptoed around Wali for a peek. So this was the famous sister. She was a pretty little thing. Eight or nine maybe, with kinky black hair that must go halfway down her back when she was standing up. Her fingers were wrapped around a rope camel. Once the "moonlit sleeping child" effect faded, Benny started to notice details. Kaheena looked half starved. Her cheekbones were poking out through her olive skin. She had some sort of infection—scaldy looking blisters and cracks surrounded her mouth. The bed itself was ancient and rusted. Probably something left behind by the Germans on their way out. It must've been for prisoners or something, because Kaheena was strapped in by two thick leather bands.

Omar started sobbing, his bony little ribcage pumping. Wali rubbed his head as gently as he could. With a hand that size it must be like trying to ring a doorbell with a wrecking ball. The girl opened her eyes, but she wasn't awake, not really. They must be giving her something. She knew Omar, though. Knew him right away. She stroked his hand, a painful smile on her lips. Omar sniffed mightily and ran a sleeve across his face, trying to put a brave face on it.

"Asslama ukht. Sh'nawalek?"

Kaheena nodded weakly, placing a hand on her heart. Omar broke down again. She was anything but fine. Kaheena held out her homemade camel. Her brother took the toy and stroked it gently.

Benny wondered if seeing Georgie in a bad state would have this effect on him. He tried to imagine the Crawler in the bed, but the image wouldn't stick in his mind.

"Hello again, Irish," said a voice behind him. He spun around, as you would when you're lurking around a foreign prison camp and you hear your own language behind you.

"Couldn't stay away, could ye?" said the voice. A gold tooth glittered in the shadows.

"Howye, Mr. Asaad."

"Hello . . ."

"Benny."

"Benny. Let's go outside and let Omar have a chat with his sister."

Benny swallowed. "You're not going to murder me or anything, are you?"

Samir laughed. "I haven't decided yet. But I could, laddie. Legally, I have every right. You're an intruder, after all."

"Yeah . . . but, I'm . . . you know."

"What?"

"Well, you know . . ."

"Oh, you mean you're white?"

"S'pose."

Samir laughed again, but you could tell he was forcing it. "Listen to me, boy. Your average Tunisian would much prefer to knock off a white boy than one of his own."

"S'pose. Listen, I'd just like to apologize for any trouble my race has caused. You know, the rainforest or whatever."

"Well, seeing as you apologized I suppose I could let you live."

"Cheers, pal."

"Welcome. Now, outside with you and let these two have a few minutes."

They sat on a flat-topped wall that penned in a few goats. Samir Asaad lit a pungent cigarette.

"All you crowd smoke," said Benny.

The Tunisian nodded. "They're cheap. Opium for the masses."

"Wha'?"

"It gives us something to look forward to."

"Your next cigarette?"

"Better than nothing. Anyway, you shut it. I haven't decided what to do with you yet."

Samir puffed away on his cigarette. After a minute, he knocked off the tip and stashed the butt behind his ear.

"Well?" he said.

"Well what?" replied Benny, stalling.

"Don't give me that. What're you doing here?"

"I came with . . . that other boy."

"Omar, you can say it. I know all about him."

"Yeah . . . I came with Omar."

"What's a rich white boy doing hanging around with a Tunisian orphan?"

"I'm not rich!" objected Benny.

"Compared to whom?"

Benny thought of what he had just witnessed and said nothing.

"So, how did you two meet?"

"We're not married, you know!" Benny still had a spark left in him.

"Keep it up, now," said Samir, patting his pockets. "I have my knife around here somewhere."

"Omar lives in a hut outside Marhaba village."

"*Walahi!* So that's where he is!"

"So, we've been paling around for the last couple of months."

"How do ye communicate?"

"He watches a lot of TV. We get by."

"So, Benny boy, do your parents know you're out swanning around Sfax?"

Benny swatted his cowlick. "'Course they do."

"I'm sure," snorted the director. "Maybe I should just phone the EuroGas plant. Tell them I've caught a little Irish sprog breaking into my farm."

"You were waiting for us, weren't you?" Benny decided that it was time to change the subject.

"I thought Omar would be around . . . and don't think I don't know what you're doing. It's Kaheena's birthday today. She's nine. Birthdays aren't such a big thing for us Muslims—but in Omar's case . . ."

"What's the deal with Omar?"

"Don't you know?"

"Bits of it."

Samir retrieved his cigarette butt and screwed it into the corner of his mouth. "It's a sad sort of story," he said, taking a deep drag. "The Ben Alis were Bedouin."

"Who?"

"The Ben Alis. Omar's family. Same name as our illustrious president."

"Righto. Proceed."

"Thank you. Bedouins are like your gypsies."

"Itinerants."

"Exactly. They're a dying breed. So Omar's mother persuaded the father to settle. They loaded the old pickup and headed into Sfax. Everything they owned was in the back of that vehicle. Sheep, turkeys, and Omar. There was no room for him in the cab." Asaad paused, blowing sparks from the tip of his cigarette.

"They were on their last trip from the camp. It was late. I suppose everyone was tired. Well, whatever happened, Omar's father just went straight across the railway tracks on the Gabes Road. I don't know if the lights were green or he just didn't check . . ."

Benny whistled.

"The parents were killed straight away. But someone pulled Kaheena out from underneath her mother. She hasn't spoken a word since. That was three years ago."

"And Omar?"

"They found him a hundred meters away with barely a scratch on him. *Al-hamdu li'llah*. It was a miracle."

"Holy God!"

"So, they were sent to me. Kaheena was chronically disturbed. It was all we could do to stop her hurting herself."

"The straps on her bed?"

"Yes. I don't have the people to watch her twenty-four

hours a day. We tried letting her up at first. But she acted violently. Tell the truth, she's been on that bed so long now that I don't know how much use her legs are anymore."

"Is she on drugs or what?"

Samir frowned. This must be a sore subject. "I have her on . . . medication. She gets very upset. Even the sound of the traffic can start her screaming. It's terrible, I know. But we're a developing country. Most of Africa is still treating mental illness with witch doctors."

"So what happened to Omar?"

"He seemed to be fine. He was sent to a closed orphanage."

"I bet he wasn't too fond of that."

Samir nodded ruefully. "He ran away after a week. They never caught him. Then again, no one tried very hard. There are too many orphans looking for beds."

"I know. Mr. O'Byrne in school at home is always saying that there are too many people that actually want an education for him to be worrying about the likes of me."

"Same sort of thing. So that's where he's been for the past three years! What's he doing for money?"

Benny squinted. "Here, you're not trying to get me to spill the beans, are you?"

"No," chuckled Samir. "If I wanted Omar, I'd have caught him long ago. He drops in every other week. I just like to know he's okay."

Benny considered it. "Fair enough, I suppose. Well, as far as I know he fixes up stuff, mopeds and that, and sells them."

"Nothing illegal, I hope?"

"Ah . . . no, nothing illegal. Then again, I don't know a whole lot about Tunisian law."

"Handy being a dummy, isn't it? That laddie'd better watch it. A couple more years and he could end up in prison."

Benny blinked. "What age is he?"

"Fourteen. He'd be fourteen now."

"Fourteen!" Benny couldn't believe it. "I mean, I'm not huge, but he's tiny!"

Samir flicked the end of his cigarette over the wall. "This is Africa, Benny. We don't all have the luxury of an ideal diet! Don't you ever watch that color TV EuroGas provided for you?"

"Sorry."

But Samir was wound up now. "You Europeans are all the same. You come over here and expect to be fawned over. You stay in your Marhaba villages and tell everyone that you live in Africa. Well, you don't! You live in a little antiseptic bubble where everything is brought in specially from home!"

"You're right."

The director remembered who he was talking to.

"*Ezzah!* Why am I talking to you? You're just a wee bairn."

"Bairn?"

"Baby."

"Arabic?"

"Scottish."

"Oh."

Samir stood, brushing off his long leather coat. "Right. It's time for you two to go before half the town is looking for you."

They went in, using the door this time. Omar was where they left him, stroking his sister's hand. Kaheena's eyes were closed, her small chest rising and falling regularly.

"*Ya*, Omar," called Samir. "*Marhaba.*" So they were welcome!

"*Asslama, Sidee* Asaad," replied Omar, pulling himself together. They shook hands and kissed cheeks.

Pleasantries exchanged, the director packed them off.

"*Emshee,*" he said, hustling the two of them out the door. Wali was inconsolable, blubbering energetically.

Omar gave him a hug too. Then Samir distracted the big bear with a boiled sweet and the two boys skipped out to the moped. There wasn't a whole lot to say. Still, Benny thought he should make the effort.

"Kaheena. Very pretty . . . ah . . . supermodel."

"Spice Girl," agreed Omar. He looked like he was on

the verge of tears again. "Miami Vice. *Mush behee*. Big problem."

Benny nodded. Those calming drugs would probably do your nut in after a while.

"Pretty Polly," continued Omar, smacking his legs. "Pretty Polly. Chief Ironside."

Benny had seen *Ironside* once. It was all about some big fat lad going around in a wheelchair. How was Omar expected to deal with all this? He was only a kid.

It was nearly a relief to get back into the murderous traffic.

Jessica Shaw was mortified. Two minutes after the first course, a *"bric à fruits de mer,"* her stomach began to cramp painfully. A deathly pallor shone through her foundation. This was not like her at all. She usually forbade herself to succumb to embarrassing illnesses. And things were only going to get worse.

First of all, she had to ask an oily waiter for the bathroom key. Then she discovered that there was already someone in the Ladies. Unfortunately it wasn't a lady.

Jessica decided not to wait. *"Merci,* Monsieur," she muttered and hurried back to the table. They would, she informed the company, have to go. Immediately.

Stuart Taft drove as fast as he dared. The official speed limit was fifty kilometers per hour. Stuart teased it up to seventy, keeping a sharp eye on the verge for the Garde Nationale.

"Ten minutes, Jessica," he called over his shoulder. "Hold on."

"I'm so sorry about this. The whole night—ruined."

Pat put an arm around her. "Don't worry about it, honey. It can't be helped."

"I know, but we haven't been out in ages."

April Taft's tanned face peeked around the headrest. "Don't give it another thought, dear. Sfax Revenge strikes us all in the first few months. Especially with the fish."

Pat cradled his wife, trying to soften the buffeting of the road. The traffic was crazy, as usual. You couldn't relax for a moment or some moped would be under the grille.

As if on cue, a moped skidded out from a mud track, powering out of the turn a second before their jeep. The Land Rover's powerful diesel engine drew them alongside the little bike. Like a lawn mower with a seat, it was. You'd wonder what the life expectancy of those two little fellows on it was.

The driver looked like a lunatic, his cheeks ballooning in the wind. He was crying, too, tears flying back over his forehead. It must be the phosphate agitating his eyes. It looked a bit like Benny's little mate. The same wiry little frame. Looked very much like him, actually. Pat's gaze shot to the passenger. The face was hidden by a shiny fez.

But he knew immediately. A man would know his own son in a gorilla suit. The battered Reeboks and Wexford jersey only confirmed it. And just as suddenly the bike was gone, veering up a tiny walkway between two butchers' shops.

"Oh God!" he croaked.

Jessica sat up. "What? What is it?"

Pat gathered his thoughts. "Nothing. I . . . ah . . . headache. Just gave me a dart."

"You'd want to lay off that beer, pal."

"Yes, Stuart, you're right, that must be it."

"Are you okay?"

"I'm fine—honestly. Fine. Just a dart, that's all."

Jessica half laughed. "What a night," she said, snuggling back down.

Pat Shaw was thinking dark thoughts. "It's not over yet," he said between clenched teeth.

George was watching *National Velvet*. It wasn't like Benny to let him pick the station. Maybe his brother was going soft in his old age. It might be nice if the two of them could actually get on for a while. Mother would like that. He'd be willing to give it a go. But Benny! He loved arguing. He'd never just say hello, or good morning. It always had to be Crawler this, or Crawler that. George could feel himself getting annoyed. Benny was such a . . . such a . . . moaner!

Things were nice here. School was really great, just

deadly. Although he shouldn't think "deadly." That was slang. But it was, though. And Mr. Rossi—Bob—was the best teacher ever. He talked to you and tried to help you with things you weren't good at. Of course, none of this suited Benny. Oh no! Nothing was good enough for his lordship. Mr. I'm-A-Hurler: whiney, sulky Bernard Shaw. Moan: it's too hot. Moan: no one likes me. Moan: I lost my ball. Whine, moan, gripe!

George had just realized that he'd be perfectly happy if it wasn't for his elder brother bullying him. And your brothers were supposed to protect you from bullies. That was the plan. The strange thing was that one time Benny had actually tackled a few hard men from the estates that were hassling George. Nobody was allowed to bully George but Benny.

National Velvet was over. George realized he hadn't even watched the last half-hour. Too busy thinking about his brother. Maybe they should talk. See if they couldn't have a truce. He crept down to Benny's room. George stuck his ear to the door like a plunger. Nothing except the pylon buzz of the crickets. Georgie paused. Did he really want a lock-up or the dreaded upper arm flesh-twist? No, he didn't. But he knocked anyway.

"Benny?" No answer. Maybe he'd nodded off.

"Bernard. You awake?" Still nothing.

"I'm coming in—all right?" He gave the handle a good

jiggle. Still no objection. He swung the door open, knocking all the way.

"Benny. I was wondering . . ."

But Benny wasn't there. George's heart speeded up like a playing card on bicycle spokes. You have to remember that underneath all that drama and that hairdo was a little kid. So what would a nine-year-old think when his brother disappears out of his room? This is a young lad recently arrived in Africa, raised on the *X Files* and Tarzan. He's going to think something awful has happened. Maybe a lion leaped in and dragged Benny off. Or it could have been a Tunisian that Benny insulted. And now the whole tribe was after him with those curvy knives.

A million convoluted and gory theories flashed through Georgie's imagination. He stepped hesitantly into the room. Even with Benny gone, the taboo of room invasion was hard to break. George checked under the bed and in the wardrobe. No luck. Maybe he'd just poke a nose out the window. Benny could be lying injured on the ground—sprawled there, weakly mouthing his brother's name. Georgie hopped up on the bed and looked out. Nothing but glow globes and giant moths.

"Bernard! Bernard? Are you there?" Georgie was trying to sound concerned rather than whiney, but it wasn't easy.

"Benny? Cop on. This isn't funny! I'm scared!"

Maybe Benny was unconscious. Georgie could just see it. His big brother with a fat drop of blood hanging off the top of his cowlick. Maybe he should climb out for a quick search.

It was a good plan, except for one thing: Georgie had the hand-eye coordination of a two-week-old baby. His brain told him to hook his leg over the aluminium sill. Unfortunately this order disintegrated as it flashed down his nerve endings. By the time the command to "raise foot" had reached Georgie's sneakers, a couple of inches were lost in the translation.

Instead of clearing the window, his sole snagged on the sill. Georgie went through the window, but his foot stayed behind. This sort of a situation would have been no problem for Benny or most young lads. A quick roll and a grazed elbow would have been about the size of it. Unfortunately, nature shares out the genes and Georgie was the actor in the family, not the athlete. So, instead of rolling himself up in a ball, Georgie fell like Wile E. Coyote off a cliff: chin out and arms flapping uselessly. It wasn't Georgie's night. The paving around the chalet was only about eighteen inches wide and he still managed to burst into it with his head.

Benny said his *m'asslamas* and took a running jump at the wall. There wasn't a whole lot of point hanging around.

Omar wasn't in the mood for chat. He wasn't rude or anything, just quiet and shifty looking.

He sprinted around the perimeter. There were a few guards clustered around the globes. No sign of the boy Mohamed, though. Maybe he was off harassing some poor innocent.

Benny snuck around to his window. Still open, the way he'd left it. He placed two hands on the sill and catapulted into his room. He landed, catlike, on the bed. Ain't it grand to be an athlete! Someone was roaring on the telly. Sort of a piggy squeak. Georgie boy couldn't be watching a horror movie or something, could he?

Suddenly Pat Shaw was in the doorway, a black figure in a white frame. "So there you are!" Da shouted. There was a ragged tinge to his voice, like the edge of a tin can that you always catch your thumb on.

I'm corpzublicked, thought Benny. And he was right. Da had him by the scruff, dragging him out to the bathroom door.

"Do you hear that, do you?"

The squealing wasn't on the TV, it was in the toilet. It was George. Benny got that "monkey swinging on his intestines" feeling.

"That's your younger brother crying in there." Benny could feel Da's breath in his ear. "D'you know why he's crying? Do you?"

Benny didn't.

"Well, do you?"

"No, Da, I—"

"Don't you try to fool me! Your nine-year-old brother is in there bawling his eyes out because he's bleeding."

"I don't—"

"Shut up! He's bleeding because he split himself falling out the window while you were supposed to be minding him. Poor Georgie was worried that something might have happened to you! Can you believe it? I could've told him that you were grand. And do you know how I know? Do you?"

Silence.

"Well, do you?"

"Uh-uh."

"I know because I saw you gallivanting around the town with your little buddy Omar!"

There was a yelp from inside. Pat Shaw's fingers tightened painfully on Benny's shoulder. "How could you do it? How could you?"

Benny didn't know. He couldn't think. He was in shock.

"Leaving him on his own! He could've been killed."

"I just—"

"Shut up! Shut your gob, Benny! None of your smart talk! Call yourself a brother? You're not a brother. Or a son. You're no part of a family. Because people in families think about each other once in a while."

This was getting scary. Benny couldn't remember ever seeing Da this angry. It made you wonder how badly Georgie had injured himself.

"It was lies. The whole lot of it. Lies. That Omar chap isn't the son of any guard."

"Yeah, but—"

"Oh don't bother with your stories. I know. I rang Mr. Khayssi. They've had trouble with him before. He's a little thief! And a vandal!"

Benny started to cry.

"Ah, here we go. Turn on the tears. Never mind the blubbering, boy. You've burnt your boats this time."

Benny didn't know what to do. What was the right thing to say? "Da, I'm sorry."

Pat Shaw laughed. A mirthless, pained snort. "Sorry! Sorry! The only thing you're sorry about is getting caught."

"No, really."

"Shut up, Benny. I'm too angry to talk to you."

Inside, Georgie kept bawling. Benny tried to wish himself invisible. For a minute it worked. Dad was breathing heavily beside him, like someone after doing laps.

There was a knock at the front door.

"That'll be them," muttered Pat Shaw. He set off at a

run, dragging his blubbering son with him. "You sit there," he said, swinging Benny on to an armchair. "Keep your trap shut and don't move an inch." He took a step toward the door, then turned back. "Don't think I'm going to forget this," he whispered. This new tone was much scarier than a roar. "I'm not going to calm down. I'm going to make myself stay angry. You are going to regret this night for a long time."

Benny was shaking. It was all George's fault, as usual. That chap couldn't even sit on a sofa properly. He had to go and fall out a window. Typical.

Talal Khayssi, the village director, was at the door. "*Asslama*," he said. "I have with me the doctor."

Doctor! What was the Crawler after doing to himself?

"Come in, come in," said Pat. "Thanks for coming so quickly."

"*Mafi mushkela*. No problem, Mr. Shaw."

They stepped into the unit, a couple of mosquitoes slipping in with them. The doctor was a fairly officious looking chap—three-piece pinstripe, thick glasses, the whole job.

"*Bonsoir,*" he said, extending a hand.

Pat Shaw took the hand. "He's down here. I think he's going to need a few stitches."

Stitches! Benny felt sick.

They disappeared into the bathroom. For a second the

true volume of Georgie's roaring escaped through the doorway. The little chap sounded like he was in serious pain. For once Benny hoped that his brother was acting.

Benny decided to chance a prayer. *Dear God,* he began. But *Dear God*—what? Everyone knew that prayers didn't work if you only used them in an emergency. There was no point in nodding off halfway through the "Hail Mary" for years and then getting all holy when you got in trouble. Maybe a prayer for someone else was okay. *Dear God,* he continued, *please let Georgie sit still for the stitches or he'll have a scar like the teeth on a saw.*

Talal Khayssi glared at Benny accusingly. "You left your brother?"

No comment.

"This boy Omar? He is trouble. No good."

Benny forced his lips together. If there had been a zip he would have used it.

Khayssi smoothed back his oiled hair. "Master Shaw, if he continues to trespass, Mohamed Gama will pay his hut a visit. He is not as diplomatic as I." A little twitch was jumping at the corner of Khayssi's mouth. Tunisian men weren't used to being defied by insolent boys.

The interrogation was interrupted by a shrill scream from the bathroom. Benny winced. The needle was going in. He knew all about stitches. Hurling did that to you. First a jab of anesthetic and then the fishhook needle.

Another yelp. That was stitch number one. Benny imagined the thread dragging after the needle. No amount of anesthetic could take away that feeling. Benny counted the screams. Seven. That was one jab and six stitches. The blood must be pumping out of him. Why couldn't he have stayed on the sofa?

The bathroom door opened. George had settled down now into a kind of hitching sob. Pat Shaw came out with the doctor. The two of them looked wrecked.

"Thanks very much, Dr. Jalil," said Da, attempting a smile. "Not much of a way to spend your Saturday night."

Khayssi stood. "Dr. Jalil has not the English. I will pass on your message."

Pat nodded. "Good. Fine. Thank you, Mr. Khayssi."

"Talal . . . please."

"Okay. Thank you, Talal."

"You are most welcome. But . . ."

"Yes?"

Khayssi took a breath. "I would like to ask that your son, Master Bernard, no longer consorts with this boy Omar. He is a thief with many bad friends. If we are not careful, there will be bands of homeless boys rampaging through our village each night. This is not a situation that I would like to see come to pass."

Da threw Benny a harsh glare. "Don't worry, Talal. It

177

will be a long time before Bernard here has any free time to consort with anyone."

Khayssi passed this on to Doctor Jalil. All three men did a round of handshakes and the Tunisians left. This was not one of those occasions where you hung around for a cup of tea. There was punishment to be doled out.

They sat together on the sofa: Ma, Da, and George. The Crawler had a padded bandage over one eyebrow. A red dot had penetrated the plaster like an inkblot. Benny couldn't take his eyes off that dot. The funny thing was that Georgie was okay now. He wasn't interested in strangling his big brother. He just wanted to go to bed. Ma and Da weren't prepared to let it go that easily.

"Well?" said Da. "Tell your mother what made you betray our trust and leave your brother."

Benny's throat felt about the width of a straw. "I know it's my fault——" he began.

"Oh listen! He knows it's his fault. Well sure, that's grand then. As long as you know. We can all toddle off to bed and forget about the whole thing."

"Ah, Ma!"

Jessica Shaw jumped to her feet. "Don't you dare! Ma! You know I hate that name! For years I've been asking you—pleading with you. But you can't even do that one little thing, can you? No. Because you're a hurler, and hurlers don't have to follow any rules." Jessica said "hurler" in a tone usually reserved for authors of bad reviews or for Adolf Hitler.

Da took over the lecture. "So this is what happens when you're asked nicely. Well, all right, then. At least everyone knows where they stand. Because I'm telling you one thing, me bucko. You'll never be asked nicely again."

"Da, it was Omar's sister."

But it was no use trying to explain. Any attempt just made his parents angrier.

"Omar's sister! Omar's sister! Oh I see. So, you have no time for your own brother but you don't mind abandoning him to toddle off to Omar's sister."

"I'm all right now, Daddy."

"Good man, Georgie. You see that, Bernard? Even with his head split open and six stitches in it, your brother is trying to get you out of trouble. You're lucky to have a brother like that. Blessed."

"I know."

"Oh you know, do you? That's why you skived off and left him, is it?"

"I didn't think—"

Mam pounced on that one. "And there we have it. You didn't think. That's the root of the problem—right there." She turned to her husband. "You finish this, Pat. I'm going to bed."

Pat nodded. "Okay, pet. You go ahead. Take George down to bed. I'll handle this fellow, don't you worry."

They went off. Nobody said goodnight. Pat Shaw rubbed his eyes and didn't speak for a long time. Benny watched his Da furtively, ready to snap his eyes back down to his feet.

Pat Shaw stood and gave his son a defeated look.

"You really played us all for a crowd of eejits, didn't you? Well, I hope you had a good laugh all those times you were sneaking out over that wall. Because your days of laughing are over. I see now that the only way to deal with you is with a firm hand. I'm too tired to think now. But in the morning I'll be giving you your new timetable."

Good, thought Benny. At the moment he felt like being kept busy. "Will I go to bed, Da?"

Pat Shaw shrugged. "Do whatever you like, Bernard. I don't care."

Benny would have preferred to hear almost anything except those three words.

10
HARD LABOR

You wouldn't think you'd be able to sleep after a night like that. You'd think that thoughts and ideas would be hopping off the inside of your head. But Benny slept all right. He dreamt that the whole family was around a long table eating dinner, and for some reason he had this urge to slip away and talk to someone. The dream didn't last long because Da woke him at the crack of dawn. He jerked the quilt off his son.

"Up," he snapped.

Benny searched for a sign that Pat Shaw had cheered up a bit, but if he had, he wasn't letting on. There was a sheet of paper on the coffee table.

"That's your new timetable," said Da. "You follow it to the letter or by God I'll make you suffer." And that was it. Pat Shaw went back to bed, leaving his eldest to brood over his duties.

Monday to Friday went like this:

7:00 A.M.—Get up. Wash. Breakfast.

7:15 A.M.—Empty dishwasher. Make school lunches.

7:45 A.M.—School.

3:00 P.M.—Break.

3:15 P.M.—Homework.

6:00 P.M.—Dinner.

6:15 P.M.—Take out rubbish. Load dishwasher.

7:00–9:00 P.M.—Study.

9:15 P.M.—Bed.

Benny blinked. That was pretty severe. No slots for hurling or even telly. He'd been grounded before but there was always a time frame. This looked like it was going to go on indefinitely. He read on:

Sat./Sun.

7:00 A.M.—Wake up.

7:30 A.M.—Physical exercise. Six laps.

8:30 A.M.—Cook fry-up for family.

9:00 A.M.—Breakfast.

10:00 A.M.—Clean up.

10:30 A.M.–2:30 P.M.—Chores.

    (Chores? That was a scary one.)

2:30–3:00 P.M.—Lunch.

3:00–4:00 P.M.—Clean up.

4:00–7:00 P.M.—Study.

7:00–8:30 P.M.—Free time.

8:30 P.M.—Bed.

This was ridiculous. How could he stick to this? It was like prison or something. And there was more.

General Rules:

1. No fraternizing with Omar whatsoever.

2. Respect will be shown to family members at all times.

3. Any complaints or refusals will result in an extra week of punishment.

An extra week? So this dictatorship was going to go on for more than one week. Everyone seemed to be over-reacting, just a bit. It wasn't as if he'd murdered anyone, just sneaked out for a couple of hours. He knew chaps that smoked, drank, and went down the back drainpipe every night. The most he deserved was a good telling-off. Maybe a light grounding.

"Benny!" The roar shook him from his little vision.

"Yes, Da?"

"Don't you Da me, Benny boy! You owe me six laps before breakfast!"

Sighing, Benny laced up his runners.

* * *

And so we enter a not-so-golden period in the young life of Benny Shaw. If you were to put backing music to this section, it'd be something all doom and gloomy. Maybe "Poor Lonesome Me" by some country-and-western chappie. It was up, work, eat, sleep. And the worst thing about the jobs was that they were all things that Khayssi's crew should be doing. A couple of blue jumpsuiters would arrive to weed the back patio and they'd find Benny on hands and knees. So the two boys would plant themselves on the patio chairs, light up their smokes, and pass comments. It was a cruel job, too, that weed pulling. There was no end to it. Bent over, with the sun bouncing off your back and your knuckles scraped from the flagstones. But the worst of it was listening to the other two snickering away behind you.

There is always great rejoicing in the world of men when a smart aleck gets his comeuppance. Not a sinner on the camp had any sympathy for Benny. Now, that wasn't exactly true. There were a couple of people who felt sorry for the little Irish chap as he pulled out the weeds or mowed the grass around the bachelor units. George was one. He would bring his brother Cokes on his break. Benny, being Benny, thought the Crawler was coming out to gloat, and accepted the refreshments with bad grace and no thanks. The other person was, believe it or not, Grace. She would peek out through the lace curtains of her bedroom, watching Prisoner Shaw perform whatever task had been set for him that day.

Talal Khayssi sent over a list of jobs that Benny could be getting on with. Thanks very much, Talal! It was mostly weeding. His favorite. So, come the weekend, Benny would be farmed out to other families to do their patios. Some had the good grace to be embarrassed, but not many.

It went on for weeks. It was more like a new way of life than a punishment. The parents were fed up waiting for Benny to become a Good Person of his own accord, so now they weren't giving him a choice. He nearly broke his parents' resolve once, though. He had them feeling sorry for him and everything. And then, of course, he had to go and blow it.

By the third Sunday, the weather was cooling off a bit, but there was still more strength in that sun than you'd ever get back home. Benny had been packed off on the ignoble errand of sweeping out roof guttering after a sandstorm. So, away he went with ladder and brush, begging the residents to let him up on their roofs. Like they were doing him a favor! Being Irish, Benny decided to do the job "à la farmer": shirt tied around the waist and back to the sun. The sneaky thing about sunburn is that it doesn't come up until later on. You think you're grand. You think that you've already got enough of a base tan to protect you. But then as soon as you try to go to sleep, the agony begins.

By seven thirty that night, Benny was in bed. He still had an hour of free time on the schedule. But he was totally wrecked after a day on the roofs.

Soon as he started to nod off, the sunburn made itself felt. Benny began to feel like an electric heater. A dull pain with crackly wrinkles flowed out across his back and legs. At first it wasn't too bad. But gradually it grew from an annoyance to excruciating agony. The pain settled down into his bones, cutting deep into creases and crevices. The sheet felt like sandpaper. He threw it off, panting. But it did no good.

Now the air seemed heavy and rough. He imagined the currents scraping across his neck. He dreamed of icy waters and soothing cream. But more than that, he dreamed of a few words of sympathy from his mother. Like that time when the St. Christopher medal she sewed into his helmet got whacked into his head, or the time when he'd stuck his foot in the bike spokes and skidded along Clonard Road on his elbows. He couldn't see himself getting any soft words tonight, though. Not from the Parents of Stone.

He must've been sniffling a bit in his sleep because Mam came in for a look. Even in the light from the hall, his back was glowing like a Sacred Heart lamp.

Benny woke and heard his ma drawing a shocked breath.

"Pat," she whispered. "Pat, come and have a look at this."

Da came, mumbling away to himself. "What is . . ." he stopped short. "Oh my God. He's like a tomato."

"I know. I'd better get some cream."

Benny could see the shadows on the wall. His Ma's disappeared. The Da shadow was flattening his cowlick. It flitted into the room. The foot of the bed sank and creaked.

"Oh, Benny," said his father. "How am I supposed to know what'll work with you? Maybe this is too much. Maybe you've been punished enough."

Ma came back. "Push up there, honey." The bed bounced again. And Benny felt the cool spread of Sudocrem across his back. He gasped. "Shh, Bernard. Don't move now."

Benny relaxed his shoulder blades, feeling the soothing lotion seep down to his bones.

"Benny. You awake?"

"Yes, Da."

"Have you been thinking about everything? About the past few weeks?"

"Yeah."

"You must know you were wrong, Bernard."

"S'pose."

"You suppose? You left your brother on his own. You risked your own life in that crazy traffic."

At that point Benny had it made. All he had to do was burst out crying or offer any sort of convincing apology and it would all have been over. It would have been group bawling and hugs all around. But no. He had to go and blow it.

"It would've been all right," said Benny, "if George had just stayed on the couch."

The hand stopped rubbing. The weight lifted from his bed.

"I should've known," said Da. "God, you never learn, do you?"

"Da?"

"Oh stop, Benny, would you? Just stop."

"Mam!"

"There's no point talking to you. None at all. You probably haven't put one minute's thought into what's happened."

"I have," protested Benny, turning over.

"'Course you have," said his Da. "Course you have."

They closed the door behind them. Benny banged his head on the pillow. Stupid! Stupid! Stupid!

Every weeknight, Benny had to come up with ways to fill in two hours of study time. Actual study was always an option, but not one he took up very often. Tried it once. Didn't like it. Back in Wexford you could always have a little nap. But here you had no creaky stairs or noisy door to tip you off that you were about to be inspected. So, at the very least, Benny had to stay at his desk.

There was nothing to watch outside the window except insects. If he was bored enough, Benny would gaze at them for ages. It was nature study, he told himself. And there he was, one Tuesday night, staring at an unfortunate stick insect, when Omar's head popped into the beam.

"Holy God!" yelped Benny, promptly falling off his chair.

This cheered Omar up no end. He chortled mightily, the lamplight turning him into a shadowy gargoyle.

"Binny. *Asslama*."

Benny recovered himself quickly. If Da heard any of this commotion there'd be murder.

"*Sh'nawalek?*"

"I'm fine. Now be quiet, will you."

"Eh?"

"Quiet. *Mafi* volume."

It was no use. You couldn't whisper through a pane of glass. Benny opened the window. "Omar. Sshh! Da is angry." No response. "Da. Grr. Grr." Plenty of frowning and grimacing.

Omar got it. "Da. David Banner Hulk."

"*Na'am*. Hulk."

"Binny. Omar. Few pucks?"

"*Laa. Mafi* pucks tonight, Omar, boy. *Mafi* pucks ever."

"Binny eejit."

"Omar *beleed*!" Standing there, getting insulted by a friend, it was easy for Benny to forget how much trouble he was in.

"Binny. Omar. Bee Gees?"

"Yeah, we're still brothers. But my real brother got bursted . . . ah . . . Georgie. Bee Gee Benny. The Crawler?"

Omar remembered him from the All-Ireland night. "Georgie Crawler."

"Yeah. The Crawler. Well, he had a little accident." Benny whacked himself on the forehead and used wiggly fingers for blood.

Omar winced. "Flesh wound. He'll live?"

"Yeah. *Na'am*. But I mightn't."

Omar hopped in the window. Just like that—he was in.

"No! Omar, no! Big *mushkela*. Da angry. Much bad juju."

"Binny eejit."

"You have to head off now, Omar," Benny whispered desperately.

"Ride off into the sunset?"

"That's it. Go on, hop it. Da's bullin'."

Omar waved a finger. "*Laa*. Da, Omar, buddy-buddy. Omar video All-Eyerland."

"That was before. He thought you were Gama's son . . . Omar Bart Gama."

Omar blanched. "*Mafi* Bart Gama! *Mush behee!*"

"I know. I know. I had to say something. Now go. *Emshee!*"

Omar smiled suddenly. A bit nervously. "Ah . . . *Sidee* Shaw."

Benny whipped his head around, nearly giving himself whiplash. Da was standing at the door.

"Good evening, Omar," he said.

"*Asslama*. Howdy pardner."

"I think you've forgotten your rules, Benny."

"No, no, honest, Da. He just showed up. I was trying to get him to go."

"I'm sure."

"Honest."

"Didn't sound like that to me."

Omar sensed the tension and thought maybe he could help out. "*Sidee* Shaw?"

"Yes, Omar?"

"Georgie Crawler. Flesh wound. Okeydokey?"

"Pardon?"

"Georgie Crawler. Flesh . . ."

"I heard what you said." Pat Shaw glared at his son. "So now you're telling other people nicknames for your brother."

"No, Da. That was from before."

"So it was okay before, was it?"

"No. Well, it was a joke."

Da scowled. "Your jokes aren't very funny lately. Now! You, Omar, it's time we had a chat with Mr. Gama."

Omar understood one word. "Gama?"

"Yes, Gama!"

"Da, don't. You don't understand."

"You keep out of it. You don't get a vote anymore."

Omar was up on the bed now. "*Laa, Sidee* Shaw. *Mafi* Gama. Gama Darth Vader."

"What's he saying?"

"He learns from the telly."

"Quiet, Benny."

"You asked me."

"I said—"

"Okay, okay."

Da stretched out a hand. "Okay, Omar. Let's go."

Omar shook his head. "*Laa, Sidee* Shaw."

"Come on, now."

"Binny?"

Benny knew he was up the creek, whatever happened. Da was going to lambaste him for having Omar in here in the first place. Ah well. "Ride off into the sunset, *sahbee*," he said.

Da frowned. "What?"

Omar got it. Missus Ben Ali hadn't raised any eejits. He nodded once and was out the window like a greyhound out of a trap. Pat Shaw knew by the speed of that exit that there was no point in pursuit.

"What was that all about?"

"He didn't know he was barred."

Da shrugged. He looked tired and harried. This punishment lark was affecting him more than his son. He sighed. "I'll leave you to pretend you're studying."

11

FREEDOM

In spite of what youngsters think, parents do not get a sneaky thrill out of punishing their children. Not all of them anyway. Pat Shaw was finding it particularly hard. Work was a nightmare. Long weeks of delays, minor explosions, and leaky pipelines were all taking their toll on the Irish engineer. Then he had to come home and give Benny the hard face. It wasn't easy.

He missed the sports chats and the headlocks. He missed thinking of his eldest son as a kindred spirit. Pat Shaw had married Jessica Mills because she was so wonderfully different. But still and all, sometimes you felt like talking to someone with the same interests as yourself. Someone who didn't care a whole lot about method acting or Alexander Solze-whatever his name was. And that was Benny. Benny was his da's mate.

One Friday in December, Pat Shaw finally cracked. He sat in the driveway with his forehead on the steering wheel. Here I am, he mused, sitting outside the house because I don't want to go in to my own family. Ah here, he thought, this is ridiculous. Pat switched off the Horslips tape and stamped into the living room.

"I've had enough of this, Jessie," said Pat, flinging his briefcase on the sofa. "Benny! Get down here!"

Nothing for a moment. Doubtless, Benny was trying to make it look like he'd been awake. Finally the eldest son appeared at the door.

"Yeah?" he muttered. There was a spirally pattern on his face from leaning against the lace curtain.

"Been watching the bugs again?"

"No, Da . . . well, a bit."

Pat pointed at an armchair. Benny sat. "This last month has been a pain for all of us. You see, you have to learn. We're trying to teach you, the best way we know how."

Jessica nodded, urging him on. Benny was trying to look interested. Pat knew what was happening. He had to suffer this look every day at work. He rubbed his tired eyes with the heels of his hands.

"I know you're not listening."

"What?"

"I know what you're doing, Benny. You're sitting there thinking: yeah, yeah, yeah, here we go again."

"I'm not, Da—"

"Yes, you are. Here's Da giving another lecture. In one ear, out the other. I know."

"Pat?"

"Well he is, Jessie! It's the whole problem. Benny never listens."

"I do."

"When it suits you, you do. Oh I know you've a big listening face that you paste on every time I'm talking. But you're not really hearing what I'm saying to you."

Benny swallowed. Da must've caught the honesty bug from Harmony.

"Wouldn't it be great if you could listen? It'd be brilliant. I'd just say something and you'd listen! There's a novel idea for you. What do you think of that one, boy?"

"Da. I'm not—"

"You'd never have to be punished. Imagine that! I'd just tell you something and you'd listen. Wouldn't that be just deadly now?"

Jessica held out a hand. "Pat?"

He took it and sat. "I know. I know. I'm just fed up with the whole thing," he sighed. "Have you learned anything, son?"

Benny considered it. "S'pose."

"Well, what then?"

"I dunno. Do what I'm told and all."

"But why, Bernard? Why?"

Benny flapped his lips for a while. This was some kind of test. "'Cause you tell me, I suppose."

The parents sighed. Wrong answer.

"Maybe he knows himself," said Jessica. "He just can't articulate it."

"Maybe," said Da, not looking at all convinced. He slapped his knees. "Right."

"What?"

"I'm giving you a chance."

Benny squinted. Often these sort of deals weren't as rosy as they first appeared. "A chance?"

"Yes, God help me."

"Pat, maybe we should discuss—"

"I know. I know. But I'm after saying it now."

"What is it, Daddy?" said Georgie. His first words so far. That swung it.

Jessica ran her thumb along the pink scar over George's eyebrow. "Go on, Pat."

"You know that school trip to the desert this weekend?"

"Yeah, but—"

"You're going."

"But Da!"

"Don't! Don't think you can start arguing with me, bucko. We're not that buddy-buddy yet."

"Okay. Sorry."

"You're going and that's it. If you can behave yourself, then we'll see about your schedule."

Benny nodded.

"But if I hear one word from Harmony or Bob about you acting the maggot . . ." Da let the sentence hang.

Benny's brain was churning away. Going on a school tour with a shower of people that hated him, or spending the weekend unplugging drains. Tough choice. Not that he had a choice. Would this be the time to try and weasel a better amnesty? Benny looked at his Da. He saw the tiredness in his face, the gray creeping up the side of his head. Maybe he should take it easy on the old man. Give him a break.

"Okay, Da. Fair enough. I'll go."

Pat snorted. "Like you had a choice! Now, hoppit down to the bedroom. You still owe me half an hour of study."

That shook Benny a bit. He thought he was off the hook altogether. "Righto, so. I'll be off then!"

"Good man. You do that."

And off he shuffled.

Jessica pulled George onto her knee, even though he was getting a bit old for that sort of thing. "We're so lucky to have you, honey."

"I know," said Georgie, smiling.

"That was a nice thing you did there."

"What was?" Georgie wasn't above fishing for compliments.

"You know very well, little man. You were trying to help out your brother."

Georgie nodded. "Well, you know, Mammy, Benny's only bold because he's not as clever as us."

Pat hung his head. "God help me. What am I raising?"

"He didn't mean it that way, did you, honey?"

"Mean what?"

"You see, Pat?"

Pat Shaw nodded weakly. "Any beer in the fridge, Jessie?"

The desert trek was kicking off on the following Friday. Two days to go. Benny could just imagine what the weekend was going to be like. Plenty of "Ging Gang Gooley," "Row Row Row Your Boat"–type songs. And they'd all go gaga down at the desert. Oh look at the sand! It's so . . . grainy. Fawn, fawn, blubber, blubber. The sand didn't care if you liked it or not. You could roar abuse at sand and it would just lie there ignoring you. Personally, Benny didn't expect to be that impressed by the Sahara. How excited could you be about dunes? It'd be just like Carne Beach without the water.

Benny stared at his watch, trying to make it go faster. Come on, he broadcast. Tick! No good. It was still only four thirty. Another ninety minutes to go before dinner. He went back to his post by the window. How could you distract yourself for that length with a view like this?

And suddenly, there was Grace. She had a white T-shirt on her, down to her knees, and blue chunky flip-flops. She gave one of the guards a wave. Benny sighed. She even waved cute, wiggling her fingers instead of the whole hand.

Grace turned into the driveway. Their driveway! His driveway! She walked right past him, up to the door. Benny flattened his face against the glass, trying to see what was going on. He felt the knock vibrating down the walls. What had he done? He couldn't remember doing anything. Cop on to yourself, Benny boy. It could be anything. She could be just looking for a cup of sugar. Don't be so paranoid.

His Ma's voice echoed down the hallway. "Bernard!"

So much for paranoia. Okay. Calm, calm. Nothing to be worried about. Just going to see a girl who'd ignored him for the past two months. Why was he worried? Who was worried? Not Benny.

"Bernard?" Ma was using her for-company voice. Sweet on the outside but with an underlying death threat. Better get a move on. He hurried down to the sitting room.

"Yeah?"

"Good. Bernard, glad you . . ." Jessica stopped, the sight of her son freezing her vocal cords.

"What is it?"

They were both staring at him now. Like he had two heads or something. Benny caught sight of his reflection in the dresser door. His hair was pointed skyward. Just on one side though. The side that he'd been resting on the desk. He smoothed it the best he could.

"Grace has called to see if you would like to go for a swim."

"Wha'?"

"A swim, Bernard. A swim."

"Oh yeah. A swim. I know . . . well?"

"Well, seeing as she called especially, I suppose we could make an exception. But you'll have to make up the study later."

"S'pose." Benny was stunned. What was going on here? Some sort of trick.

"Well, go on. Get a towel. And your suit. The good ones, now! Not that old rag with the anchor on the pocket."

"Suit and towel. Yeah. Right." He skipped off down to the wardrobe before either female changed her mind.

This was a big day for Benny. Freedom from the house. A possible reconciliation with Grace Taft, and his first dip in the pool. This was one of those days you remembered forever. He was being so careful not to do anything wrong that he didn't even speak for ages.

Grace lifted the child lock off the pool gates and ran in ahead of him. She threw off her T-shirt and dived in, right out of her flip-flops. That was nifty, thought Benny; he could never do something like that. Her water-fractured shape rippled to the other side before breaking the surface.

"Oooh," she squealed. "It's getting chillier now. Still, you wouldn't be swimming in November at home."

Benny smiled politely. No time for small talk. He had to figure a cool way to get into the pool.

"Come on, Bernard!"

She was imitating his mother! The wee devil. He pulled off his sneakers and took a running dive. Chilly? It was warm! He'd never been in water this warm outside of a bath. Bubbles pelted him, bursting up through his fingers and toes. There was no way he was surfacing before reaching the other side. It seemed a lot further away now. Probably something to do with light being bent. Eventually his scrabbling fingers touched the tiles. He came up, trying to breathe casually.

"That's not cold," he gasped. "I thought you'd be used to cold water. The North Sea and all."

"I never actually swam in the North Sea, Benny," said Grace, holding on to the side with her elbows.

They were quiet for a while. Until Benny eventually screwed up his courage.

"Sorry about the dress and everything," he muttered, half into the water.

"That's okay. Forget about it."

"Great."

"What's the story at home?"

"I'm out on bail. If I behave on the desert weekend then I might get a pardon."

Grace laughed, with her little snort at the end. "It's not that bad."

"Oh, really."

"Really. We had good fun in Douz last year."

"Doing what?"

"Well, we went on camel rides. Then there was a disco. They have two pools with a slide. And the quads were good."

"Quads?"

"Those little motorbikes with the bubble wheels."

"That doesn't sound too bad," admitted Benny.

Grace slid underwater and swam another width. Halfway across, the pool timer hit five o'clock and the underwater lights flashed on, turning their wavy bodies white.

"Why'd you come by?"

"Dunno. Just did."

"I thought you all hated me."

"No one hates you." She squinted, trying to think of the words. "You came into school like you already hated us before you even met us."

"I did not."

"People are just friendly. You don't have to be so sarcastic all the time."

"'Course I do."

"Why, though?"

"Because . . . well . . . that's just the way everyone is. If I'm not doing it to you, you'll be doing it to me."

"No, we won't."

"Really?"

"Really. We don't have to."

"Why, though?"

Grace scowled. Even her patience had its limits. She kicked off toward the shallow end. Benny dived underneath, scraping his chest on the blue tiles. He flipped over and waved up at Grace. The pressure forced the oxygen out of his lungs and he surfaced. Grace was floating on the top, her toes tucked into the ladder.

"Y'see, Benny, Americans are different to us. These ones, anyway."

"Who are you tellin'?"

"No, Benny. I mean they're nice. They're not used to someone like you passing smart comments all the time.

You just have to be yourself with them, that's all."

"Sure, I am meself. Who else could I be?"

Grace took a mouthful of water and fountained it over her head. Very ladylike. "I dunno, Benny. I think you're afraid to be yourself in case no one likes you."

"Oh, very clever," snorted Benny. "I think you're hanging around with too many Americans. I don't believe any of that psychowhatshisface."

Grace smiled a little smile. "Is that right?"

"Yes, that's right!"

"So how come the first day you got here, you snuck off without saying a word."

"So? Hey! I thought we were being nice here."

"You're a Celt. You can take it."

Benny felt the warm water swirling about his legs. He saw Grace's smooth profile dipping up and down.

"Yeah. Suppose I can."

"So what happened with you and that other wee lad?"

"Who—Omar?"

"Is that his name?"

"Yeah. He lives outside the wall in a little hut. Da didn't like the idea of me haring around Sfax on the back of his bike."

"Nasty cut poor Georgie got too."

"Poor Georgie."

"Well he did, Benny."

"Don't you start, Grace. I get enough of this at home."

"Yeah. Well, Georgie has a big scar on his head."

"All he had to do was stay on the sofa."

"The cheek of him getting up like that."

"Grace!"

"I thought this was the way you liked talking."

Benny latched his toes around the hot water vent. He was starting to get the idea. "Righto. I'll give it a go."

"What?"

"Y'know," he made a girly face, "being nice."

"That's very big of you."

"That's the sort of guy I am."

Grace unhooked her feet, letting them sink beneath her. "Maybe we could sit together in the jeep."

"What? Ah . . . sure. Great."

Grace blushed a bit. "Just, you know, so people start talking to you again."

"Oh . . . righto."

"Some of my huge popularity might rub off on you."

"Ta very much." Benny was grinning. He couldn't help it. It seemed as though Grace liked him in spite of himself.

"Oh, and I've something for you."

"What?" Things were really looking up.

Grace smiled shyly. "This." She grabbed Benny by the ears and dunked him before he had time to shut his gob. She held him down, too, no problem. This girl was stronger than she looked. Benny could hear her laughter warbling down through the bubbles. Eventually she released him.

"Holy God, Grace," he spluttered. "You've watched *Braveheart* too many times."

But Grace was gone out of his reach, swimming elegantly to the deep end. "That's for ruining my dress," she called over her shoulder.

Benny coughed up a lungful of water.

Grace rolled out of the pool and grabbed her T-shirt. "See you tomorrow, Benny. And remember . . . be nice."

"Like you, you mean."

"Exactly."

And off she went. Benny watched her, still grinning like an eejit. He wasn't exactly sure what was going on. One minute he was the scum of the earth, and the next he was basking in a warm swimming pool, talking to what he supposed was a pretty sort of a girl. If you cared about that sort of thing.

Benny dragged himself out of the pool. His saturated shorts hung off him like builder's jeans. The evening was nippy now, with the sun behind the wall. Omar was behind there, too. Probably wondering what had happened to his friend.

Benny toweled his head. There was nothing he could do about it. If he disobeyed Da again, there'd be no telling what would happen. Anyway, this trip to Douz didn't sound too bad. Four hours sitting beside Grace and her popularity. Benny smiled through his shivers. It nearly made up for having to put up with Zoe, Heather, Ed, and James.

12
BREAKOUT

Benny got really close to going. He had the sandwiches, the flask of tea, spare vests and underpants all packed away in his gearbag. And he was looking forward to the trip too. Well, he was looking forward to the sitting-with-Grace part. If nothing else, at least he was getting out of a couple of days' slave labor. The parents bade him a fondish farewell after school on the Friday.

"You know now this is your last chance, don't you, son?"

I love you too, thought Benny. "Yes, Da," he said humbly.

"Ah here!"

"What, Da?"

"I get very worried when you start 'Yes Da'-ing me like that. I always think you're up to something."

At one time Benny would have said, up to where? But not today. Today he was taking no chances.

"Look, here's a few bob. You might have to get a round"—Jessica elbowed her hubby—"of Coke. A round of Coke."

"Cheers, Da. I appreciate it."

"You'd better."

"I do."

"Good."

Jessica decided to have a few words. She straightened the collar of Benny's Puma windbreaker.

"Bernard."

"Yes, Mam?" Good move. Not calling her Ma should win him a few brownie points. Jessica knew what her eldest was up to, but when you're a parent, you're a sucker even when you're perfectly aware you're being suckered.

"This is your chance to earn back our trust."

Benny swallowed. "Yeah. I'm sorry about George's head. I've been thinking about it and all. That's a nasty old scar he has there, too. I know how a lash like that feels." He was trying to look contrite. After years of getting in trouble, he'd plenty of practice.

Da squinted suspiciously. "Well, all right, then."

They'd swallowed it. Who said he had no acting talent?

"Off you go, then. But remember this."

Here we go.

Da scratched his chin, contemplating his words

carefully. "Whenever you find yourself tempted to stray into the territory of smart aleckry or unscheduled trips . . . just remember the past few weeks. That should dampen your enthusiasm for illegal ventures."

"Listen to your father, honey."

"Yes Ma . . . Mam, I will."

Jessica reached under her T-shirt. "Bernard. I want you to take this." It was a masks lockety thing.

"I dunno, really."

"I know, honey. You're a bit wary after the St. Christopher's."

Benny nodded, rubbing the scarred nub on his crown.

"I just want you to have something physical," said Jessica, slipping the pendant over his head. "The mask will remind you of me, Bernard."

Oh great. More guilt. This was doubtless a trick supplied by one of the women's group hippies.

"Well, I'll see yez then." He'd better head off before they gave him a set of rosary beads.

"Right so. Off you go." Da wasn't convinced. You could hear it in his voice.

"Give me a kiss, honey." Now there was a blast from the past. Ma gave him a kiss on the cheek that was more noise than contact. "Bye, then."

"I'll be back Sunday evening."

"I know. Go on. They'll be waiting."

Benny thought of the empty seat beside Grace. "Yeah, I'd better head."

He hurried off, feeling his parents waving at the back of his head. The other kids were already at the school. They'd only had an hour to get ready after class. Bob wanted to hit Douz before dark. Grace was waving at him from the fence. She was wearing dungarees and heart-shaped sunglasses. Benny waved back.

"Binny!"

Funny how he could hear her from this distance. She must be projecting or something.

"Binny! *Sahbee!*"

His brain knew it was Omar. But just for a second his hopes allowed him to ignore it.

"*Asslama*, Binny."

"Where are you, y'eejit?"

Benny couldn't see anyone offhand. He glanced around, sort of casual-like. Ma and Da were just shutting the front door. The other kids were all loading stuff into the back of a Land Cruiser. They were singing already, for God's sake. Probably a little furry-animal-we-love-you ditty. But for the moment there were no eyes on him.

Benny knew what he should do. The drama masks around his neck were telling him. Keep walking, Bernard. At least go two hundred yards without getting yourself in trouble again. Just let on you can't hear anything and make a beeline for the school.

"Binny! *Khouya!*"

Ah here. That wasn't fair. Omar was reminding him that they were brothers.

"*Khouya*. The Bat Cave."

Benny stopped. What choice did he have, really? Not a whole lot. I mean, you had to have a bit of loyalty toward your buddies. And at Benny's age that sort of thing is more important than school or having a laugh, and sometimes, though it sounds terrible to say it, even your family.

"Where are you?"

He didn't have to ask, really. He was just half hoping that Omar wouldn't answer. Some hope of that: like something was going to go right for Benny Shaw this century!

"*Uskut*, Binny! Turn down the volume!"

Good idea, seeing as half the northern hemisphere was after Omar's scalp. He was in the vacant bachelor unit, poking his nut out of the gasbox.

"Binny, *shuf!*"

"I see ye. I see ye! Shut up, I'm coming." Don't do it, said the masks, think of your parents. Benny ignored them. Oh here we go, he thought. I'm ignoring a lump of silver-plated steel.

Throwing the gearbag ahead of him, the Irish boy vaulted the wall.

"Omar," he began. "I'm under a bit of pressure at the minute . . ." But he was talking to a hole in the wall. Omar had disappeared back into the house, taking the gearbag with him.

"Well, I suppose I could stay for just a sec, seeing as you asked so nicely," muttered Benny, crawling into the gasbox.

Omar was waiting in the kitchen.

"What sort of a fool are you, Omar? Gama and his men are going crazy looking for you."

Omar wasn't paying him a blind bit of notice. He was digging food from the gearbag. "Hovis. *Behee*. Mars a day. *Behee*."

Benny had never seen him like this before. He was wild looking. His eyes had a bit more white in them than usual.

"Omar! What's the story?"

The Tunisian waved a sandwich at him. "*Shokran*, Binny. Clingfilm seals the freshness in."

"Yeah. I suppose. So what?"

But it was no use. He had to wait until his friend had finished the sandwich. Then he rooted out a can of Coke. "*Mafi* Pepsi? The choice of a new generation."

"No. *Mafi* Pepsi, smart aleck. Your majesty will have to make do."

Omar shrugged and popped the can. Down it went in one go. 'Course, after that he nearly blew himself up with a burp.

"Al-hamdu li'llah," he breathed, a bit of the madness going out of him.

"So, what're you doing here? How come you're not in the shack?"

Omar stared blankly at him. "Pass," he said.

"Ah . . . shack. Your house."

"Our house, in the middle of our street," intoned Omar wisely.

"Na'am. Yes! Your house." Benny made the international both-hands-over-the-head symbol for house.

"Mafi our house."

"What?"

"Mafi our house. Gama, our house blown to kingdom come. Big *mushkela.*"

So that was it. Mohamed and the jumpsuit gang had done a little job on Omar's pad. Perfectly justifiable in their eyes, seeing as most of it had belonged to EuroGas in the first place. That explained why Omar was in the village. The poor chap had nowhere else to go. Gama would never suspect him of being cheeky enough to camp out under his nose.

Benny tapped his watch. "I have to head off now, buddy. Okay?"

"Sh'nawalek, Binny?"

"I'm grand, boy. But I have to make tracks." Benny jerked a finger toward the hole.

"*Laa. Mafi* make tracks, *khouya*. *Shuf.*" The little chap crawled off down the corridor to the bedrooms.

"*Shuf* what? I don't have time to be looking at anything!"

Omar turned with a finger to his lips. "*Uskut*," he hissed.

"What? Am I going to wake the bugs? Well, *pardonnez-moi*!" Benny was finding that French was a great language for sarcasm. Omar cracked open the bedroom door, sneaking his head in the gap.

"Don't tell me you've brought back one of those madman soccer dogboys?" said Benny.

But a part of him knew who was in that room. And the thought of it was giving him that lurchy, top-deck-of-the-ferry feeling in his belly. What had Omar done?

"What have you done? Don't tell me . . . don't tell me . . ." He pushed past his friend into the boxroom. There she was, lying, dead to the world, on the bed.

"Kaheena," said Omar, a big soppy grin on his gob. "*Marhaba* Kaheena."

"Oh no! Oh that's it. We're well and truly sunk now. We're for the high jump this time."

"High jump. Carl Lewis," said Omar.

Benny slid down along the wall. He had so many problems now that it wasn't even funny. That eejit Tunisian had kidnapped his own sister from the Psychotic Farm.

Could you do that, he wondered? Kidnap your own sister? Maybe there was no law against it in Africa. Men being the bosses and all that.

"We're doomed," he sighed into his hands. "Utterly corpzublicked."

"Corpzublicked?" said Omar.

Benny ran a finger across his throat and then shot himself in the head with his fingers.

"Ah . . . corpzublicked. *Naraf*." Omar draped an arm around his suicidal buddy. "Binny."

Benny could tell by the tone that Omar was in serious mode. "Yeah. *Na'am?*"

"Kaheena. *Ukht*. Lisa."

"I know she's your sister."

"*Na'am*. Sister." He patted his legs. "Big *mushkela*."

"I know. It's a real problem. But if they had let her up, she might have gone crazy."

Omar nodded. "*Na'am*. Klinger section eight."

"You've got to bring her back. Back to Samir."

"Samir *sahbee*."

"Yeah, he seems like a sound enough sort of a chap. It's not his fault, you know. He's okay."

"*Na'am. Sidee* Asaad okay."

"So what's the problem?"

"Problem cocaine vice squad. *Mafi* run like the wind."

"Yeah. Them drugs are a curse."

217

"Curse of the werewolf," agreed Omar.

"Is that why Kaheena doesn't speak?"

"Pass."

"Kaheena . . . *Mafi* volume?"

Benny felt his friend's thin frame shuddering. You had to hand it to the little lad. Here he was, penniless, starving, with a shower of ugly looking guards just dying to boot him into orbit, and all he could do was worry about his baby sister.

"*Mafi* volume," he sobbed. "*Mafi* run like the wind. *Mush behee*. Binny."

Omar stumbled to his feet, trying to get a grip on himself. He stroked the sleeping girl's cheek. Her brow wrinkled and she moaned softly.

"Nightmare on Elm Street," said Omar. He pulled the blanket down. "*Shuf*, Binny."

Benny was nearly afraid to go over and look. You wouldn't know what sort of state this kid was in. Plus, he'd only ever seen her from the neck up.

"*Shuf*," repeated his friend.

So Benny went over. What choice had he? "Lord God tonight!"

The poor girl's legs were wasted away. Just two sticks with golf-ball knees and beanbag feet.

Benny took a step back. It occurred to him suddenly that this was Real Life. Not sulking or hurling or telly. But actual life-and-death type stuff. He wasn't ready for this. He wanted to go back to being a grumpy Irish boy who didn't care about anybody besides himself. Benny was getting really scared. Not just the hot and cold pins and needles "slightly worried" that he used to think was scared. But the type of scared that opened every pore in your body, boiled you up like a deep-fat fryer and took away control of your motor functions.

"Oh God. What am I going to do?"

"I'm so in love with you," completed Omar.

Benny rubbed his scalp. The cowlick was sticking up like a fishhook. "A plan, Omar boy. We need a plan."

Omar held up a crafty finger. "Plan A," he winked.

"Good . . . good. Ah . . . *behee*. Go on, tell me. I'm all ears."

Omar leaned in until their heads were touching. "Plan A. Omar, Kaheena *okond* loony."

"That's Arabic, eejit. *Mafi* Arabee. Speak telly."

"I beg your pardon."

"Well all right, then."

"I never promised you a rose garden."

Benny scowled. MTV had a lot to answer for.

Omar tried again. "Kaheena, Omar . . ."

"Yes."

"Marhaba billage."

"Village."

"*Na'am*. Village." Omar clapped his hands.

"That's it? That's the plan? Kaheena, Omar, Marhaba village?"

"*Na'am*. Plan A *behee*."

"No, no. Plan A certainly is not *behee*. It's no good, actually. *Mush behee!*"

Omar was a bit insulted. "*Laa mush behee*, Binny!" He listed off the pros: "Marhaba Ready Steady Cook. Marhaba Relax in a Radox Bath. Marhaba Southfork." And then the trump card. "Marhaba TV, *Al-hamdu li'llah*."

Benny frowned. Your man had a point, all right. They had all the comforts here. A kitchen, bathroom, beds to kip down in, and, of course, the telly. It made sense in a fairy-story-can't-see-past-your-nose kind of a way.

"Ah . . . there's just this one thing, Omar," he said guiltily. "We have a problem."

"Houston, we have a problem? *Mafi* problem."

"Yes, Omar. We do. Samir Asaad."

Omar shook his head patiently. "*Laa. Laa mushkela*."

"You don't understand, Omar. I told Samir where you lived." Benny felt lower than a snake's bum. How could he have been so daft? Rule number two of the young lads' handbook: Never tell nobody nothin'. Just after rule number one: If you believe that you're never wrong, then you never are. "Don't you understand? Benny talk talk Samir Marhaba."

Omar filtered this through the translation process. His face fell. "Binny. *Laa!*"

"I'm sorry, Omar. Honest to God!"

The Tunisian was stunned. "*Laa!* Binny!"

"I know. I'm an eejit. *Beleed*."

Omar's eyes hardened. "No. *Mafi beleed*."

"I am."

"No. Binny Judas!"

"What?"

"Binny Romulan."

"Hang on there, now——"

"Binny Jabba the Hutt!"

"Omar, stop it now. I said I was sorry."

"Binny Hannibal Lecter!"

It was all the excuse that Benny needed to forget his guilt. He could be angry instead. "Right then," he spluttered. "If that's the way it is."

"*Emshee,*" said Omar, a big sulky face on him.

"Fair enough. I will go. See how long you'll last on your own. You'll be back at the farm by lunchtime."

"*Uskut.*"

"I will not shut up! You've no right to call me a Romulan just because I made a mistake."

"Binny Ferengi!"

"Watch it, now! I've seen *Star Trek*. I know what a Ferengi is."

Omar did the one thing that could wind Benny up even more. He turned his back on him and returned to his sleeping sister.

"Fair enough. If that's how you want it." Benny slung his gearbag over his shoulder. "And don't think I'm going to come crawling back here. 'Cause I won't."

He stormed off, feeling like a balloon with just one puff too many inside it. Omar had no gratitude in him, after all Benny had done. He'd selflessly shared his sandwiches, shown him how to hurl, and heaps of other stuff. The nerve of some people.

He wiggled out through the gasbox. He'd go on the tour. He'd have a good time and that Omar could go crawl up a lamppost with his underpants on his head, for all Benny cared. How was he supposed to know that his little chat with Asaad would lead to this? Lead to what? It hadn't led to anything yet. That Ben Ali chap was having a fit over nothing.

They were waiting for him outside the school. Grace was sitting on the jeep's tailgate, swinging her legs.

"Benny," she called, waving at him.

Y'see. There now. He didn't need Omar. He had friends. Real normal people, sort of like himself. Good boy, said the masks, now you're doing the right thing, Bernard. Shut up, he thought, forgetting he was ignoring them. That boy Omar was just trouble, Bernard. Best to let him sort out his own life. You just leave off Omar, responded Benny. He was a good hurling buddy. I'd like to see you living in a hut on your own, he challenged the masks.

Ah here, he thought, this is getting ridiculous. I'm talking to meself now. He waved back at Grace, trying to force a smile. He jogged over, putting a little distance between himself and Omar.

"Where've you been?" She pronounced it "bin."

"Oh, nowhere."

"Bob thought we were going to have to send in the troops."

"Why's that?"

"Well, one minute you're there. The next . . ."

Benny shrugged. "Serious personal problems."

"Gotcha," nodded Grace. "Leprosy or foot odor?"

"Har de har har."

"Are we still on for our deal then, Bernard?" She was imitating his ma again.

"Watch it now, you. What deal?"

"You know. Being nice and all that."

"S'pose."

"Even to Heather?"

"I'll do me best. Can't promise anything."

The rest of them streamed out of the school, loaded with coolers and water bottles. Bob and Harmony had really out-hippied themselves for the occasion. Harmony had on an electric blue kaftan and a straw hat. Bob was sporting those German-type shorts and cowboy boots. Benny found it almost painful trying to suppress a snarky comment. Grace gave him a kick in the leg to help.

"Okay, you guys. I think we got ourselves a genuine photo opportunity here. Everybody in front of the jeep."

They crowded into the frame, happily huddling together. Even Benny somehow got entangled. Let go, he told himself, just give in to it.

"Hey, Benny," said Bob. "Show me those pearlies, buddy. Don't worry, be happy."

"Benny!"

"Huh?"

"I said smile!"

"Oh yeah, sorry." He pulled the corners of his mouth outward. That should do Harmony.

"Got it. A beauty. You guys are so photogenic. Darned if you don't all end up at the Oscars."

Zoe rolled her eyes. "The Oscars! They're so, like, institutional. I wanna go to Sundance."

Harmony reached into the folds of her kaftan and pulled out the triangle. She hardly ever had to ding it anymore. Just the sight of it was enough to make everyone stay quiet and listen.

"Now, I wanna talk to you guys for a minute."

Oh God, thought Benny, here we go, more hippie looking-for-yourself stuff.

"We're all going on a journey together. And I mean that in more ways than one. I want you to see this trip as more than just a drive down some dusty road. See it as a journey into yourself."

Hey, Benny wanted to shout. I'm not even thirteen yet. I'm too young for all this soul-searching bit.

"Whenever you spend time with a group of people, you have the opportunity to become truly one with the group. Drop that mask you're wearin'. Let's see what the real you looks like."

Benny got the feeling that Harmony was directing this little speech directly at him.

"Hey, Benny boy," said Harmony, her eyes huge and sad. "You know I'm talkin' to you."

"I was thinking that all right," grunted Benny.

Bob took the pipe out of his gob. "This ain't just a road trip, compadres. This is a mission. And I'm givin' it a name: Operation Clean Slate!"

"Cool!"

"Right on, Zoe! So we're all startin' over. Coming together with no preconceptions. So I'd like to say: hi, my name's Bob."

Harmony kissed his cheek. "Well, hi there, Bob. My

name's Harmony. And I hope you don't mind me sayin', but you're a fine-lookin' man."

They all giggled. Except one. Guess which one.

"Hi there, stranger," said Grace. "My name's Grace."

Benny shook her hand. "Pleasure, Grace," he said. "I'm Frank Sinatra."

"Benny!"

"How did you know that? Have we met before?"

"Don't make me slap you, Shaw!"

"Okay. Hi, my name's Benny."

"Is that short for Bernard?"

In spite of himself, Benny grinned. "I'm going to tell my ma you keep imitating her."

Harmony dinged. "Okay, people. I think you get what I'm trying to tell you. Because I don't want any negative vibes on this trip. So, what's my name?"

All: "Harmony!"

"And what do I want this weekend?"

All, even Benny: "Harmony!"

"Right on! Now let's saddle up and get this show on the road."

So they packed into the jeep. Benny climbed in beside Grace and buckled up. Bob slapped the steering wheel a couple of times until it was cool enough to hold. Then he swung out for the gate. Everyone settled instantly into travel mode. Expats spend a lot of time in cars. Zoe plugged herself into a Discman. James started in on a Tupperware bowl of chicken, and Heather and Ed cooperated on a crossword.

"What's going on up there?" wondered Grace.

Benny glanced ahead. Someone in a pickup was trying to get into the village. Gama would roll him into a ball and dropkick him over the olive grove.

"Maybe the revolution has started. This guy is a distraction while his buddies come over the wall."

"There you go, Bernard," said Grace. "A whole sentence without insulting your classmates."

"Kudos to you, buddy," said Harmony.

What in the name of God were kudos?

Those boys were really going at it. Plenty of fist waving and roaring. Bob had to pull the jeep over. No one was going in or out until that pickup was shifted. Eventually, Gama arrived on the scene. You could tell by the head on him that he was in the mood for some bone breaking.

"I wouldn't like to be the driver," said Grace.

"You're telling me."

The driver, however, was unbowed. Not only did he not back up, but he got out of the cab. Benny's happy thoughts went out the window. "Oh no!" Slicked-back hair, leather coat, glint of gold in his teeth. Samir. In search of the Ben Alis!

"What's wrong, buddy?"

"Ah . . . nothing, Missus Rossi—Harmony."

"You sure?"

"Yes!" Benny's thoughts wouldn't stay still long enough for him to get a hold of them.

"Are you sick?"

"No, Bob! I'm . . . yes, I'm feeling a bit dodgy, all right. Maybe a bug or something. I just need a bit of air maybe."

Grace shouldered open the door. "Well, hop out then. You are looking a bit pale."

Benny tumbled into the light. They were still having it out at the gate. Once Benny's name was mentioned, Gama would be after him quicker than a shark that's just spotted a stray swimmer.

Right, what were his options? There was the attractive one: get back in the jeep, keep his noggin down and head off out to the desert. By the time he got back it would all be over. Tempting. But what would happen to Omar?

So he had to warn Omar. Just trot over to the bachelor bungalow and give his buddy a few minutes' headstart. It was a minor infraction of the Gospel According to Da. But he could put up with another week of confinement in his quarters to buy off his conscience. Okay, okay, it could work: boo hoo, I have to run to the loo, just hang on a minute. Okay, Benny dude, they'd say and sing a little happy song. Then trot trot trot. Omar, danger, danger. Trot trot trot back again. Here I am, let's go. A simple plan, but a good plan. In retrospect, an extremely dopey plan.

"Ah . . . here, Bob. I have to dart off to the jacks . . . ah, loo."

Bob jiggled his pipe. "Take your time, son. We got quite a brouhaha going on between those Too-nee-shans."

Brouhaha didn't quite cover it. The two boys were up on their toes now. Maybe if Samir and Mohamed started belting each other, he wouldn't have to do anything. 'Course, soon as he thought this, the two boys froze in mid-row.

Oops, thought Benny, my name's come up. He swung his gearbag up on his shoulder and ran across to the chalets. Phase one: warn Omar. They were opening the gate and letting Samir in. Benny pumped his fists in long arcs, lengthening his stride. The pickup was on the other side of the family units, running parallel with him. How come, Benny thought between puffs, that every time I'm running, there's always someone coming after me? The vehicle skidded on gravel. They were at his house now. Benny had to veer away then, so he couldn't hear anymore. He couldn't hear them banging on the door. Or the disappointed tone in his da's voice.

He sprinted around the corner. B-twelve. Here we go. Benny went over the wall in a sort of jumpy roll. He threw his shoulder up onto the red brick and his momentum took the rest of him over. Unfortunately, he belly flopped on the concrete, skidding backwards on his stomach.

The gasbox was open. He wiggled through like a ferret down a hole.

"Omar! Ya, Omar."

No response. Obviously he was being ignored. This was no time for bad moods, Benny thought, disentangling himself from the kitchen units. The Tunisian boy was still in the bedroom, leaning over his sister.

"Omar. Come on. You've got to get out!"

He spun the boy around by the shoulder. Benny expected to get a blow or at the very least a big angry face. But Omar didn't have it in him. He couldn't even maintain a sulk. There was only room in his head to worry about his sister. His face was pale underneath the grime and his eyes wobbled in their sockets. He looked about fifty.

"Binny," he sighed. And Benny knew they were friends again.

"Big *mushkela*, Omar boy. Samir is here!"

Omar came to, like he'd put his finger in a socket. "*Sidee*, Asaad! Marhaba village?"

"*Na'am*. Yes! Yes!"

Omar roused his sister gently. Her eyes flickered, then opened. She was wild looking, like an infant that'd toddle out into the traffic without two brain cells ever colliding.

"Kaheena," said Omar. *"Andee mushkela."*

Kaheena said nothing. Like she hadn't for three years. If Mothercare had seen what Omar did next, they would have hired him on the spot for their design team. Stripping off the EG jumpsuit that he'd somehow acquired, he slipped Kaheena into the body and granny-knotted the arms and legs. A zip, a heave, and two steps later Kaheena was latched onto her brother like some sort of weird marsupial.

"Shuf," he said, grinning for the first time in ages.

"Nifty!"

"Beam us up, Scotty."

Benny nodded. "Time to get a move on."

There was no way they'd have the time to maneuver out the escape tunnel. Instead, Benny jumped up on the bed and opened the window. "C'mon. Let's go."

Omar's new passenger hadn't cost him any of his mobility. He was on the bed and out the window without touching the frame. Benny went after him.

"Benny."

"What?"

"Benny!"

Benny? Omar never called him Benny.

Grace was standing there with her hands on her hips, giving him a less-than-friendly look. "We had a deal."

"I know." There was no time for this.

"So you're just going to run off with this chap?"

"There's a whole heap going on here that you don't know about, Grace."

Grace pointed a stiff finger at him. "I knew you were lying! Knew it! You got that shifty little eyebrow thing. And you were looking at your feet."

"What eyebrow thing? Anyway, I'm not heading off. I'm just going as far as the wall. I'll be back in a minute."

"Well, your seat will be gone." She glared at Omar. "What's the matter with him? Is he pregnant?"

"No, that's his sister, Kaheena."

"His what?"

"It's a long story. We haven't time now."

"Asslama," said Omar. He tried to bow and nearly ended up flat on his face. "The name's Bond. James Bond Omar."

Grace giggled. "He's very charming for a vandal."

"Binny, *feesa!"*

"I know, I'm coming."

They heard a clamor in the distance. *"Sahbee!* Let's rock and roll. Hi ho, Silver!" Omar couldn't wait any longer. He was off, bursting down toward the squash courts.

"Grace. I have to go!"

"Why? He can't run any faster with you there."

Benny started running, shouting back over his shoulder.

"The wall! He won't make it over the wall carrying the young one."

"The what?"

"The girl!" He sprinted off, muttering to himself. "God almighty. You'd think those Scotch would learn English."

"You don't speak English," said Grace.

Benny nearly fell off his feet with the shock. Grace was keeping pace with him. No problem to her. "And it's not Scotch. It's Scott-ish."

This was embarrassing. Wouldn't the boys at home laugh at this one! A girl keeping up with him. And talking at the same time.

The village was wide open. It was like running across Holland or something. The guards were coming from all sides. With their blue jumpsuits on, they looked like iron filings. And Omar was the magnet. Samir was going round the ring road, still in his pickup. A couple of the lazier guards had hitched a ride in the flatbed. They began to suspect that this mightn't have been the greatest brainwave they'd ever had, when Samir hammered over the first speed bump.

On the other flank, you had Mohamed Gama and his cohorts all roaring into walkie-talkies. Benny wondered who they were talking to. The whole lot of them seemed to be running together. The gym! There was always one at the gym. They must be trying to wake him up.

Omar was doing his best, but how long could you

motor on with a ninety-pound limpet hanging off your neck? Benny went into high gear, digging his Reeboks into the gravel, giving it as much effort as he could muster. Grace matched him step for step. They caught Omar under the armpits.

"Warp drive," grunted Benny.

Omar just nodded. He couldn't speak. The pickup's grille was facing them now. It was like a big steely set of choppers bearing down on them. Samir's features came into focus over the wheel. Benny could see all of the director's teeth. That probably wasn't a good sign.

Behind them, Mohamed Gama's long legs were covering meters at a step. He wasn't trying to marshal the troops anymore. He was going to catch Omar himself. Sweat was coming down off Benny's forehead in sheets. Thank God for bushy eyebrows.

The gym loomed ahead. There was a guard by the path, blocking their route into the building site. Benny knew this chap. One of Mohamed's favorites. A big bogman with a beard and a distinct absence of front teeth. As if that wasn't bad enough, the guy's parents had saddled him with the name Turki.

Turki spotted them and straddled the path like a sumo. Benny broke off from the group.

"Hey, Turki," he shouted, delighted to be able to use his snarky tone again.

Turki growled, spitting out his cigarette. It wasn't often you got the chance to legitimately trounce one of those Europeans. Benny ran straight for him. The guy was reminiscent of a Bridgetown fullback he'd once played against. One swipe of those hairy fingers would snap you in two.

Benny danced around him, dodging in and out of his grasp. It was another one of his famous open-ended plans. You run in, and then you . . . well, you think of something before Turki crushes your skull like Odd Job with a golf ball. Grace and Omar had struggled past, so at least he'd accomplished that much. Benny was in the middle of congratulating himself when Turki got a hand on his head. It fitted on there like a plunger. He had visions of his eyes popping with the pressure. Time for a bit of creative fouling.

Benny's personal favorite foul was the reverse bum hunch that he'd used on Gama. Not only effective, but humiliating for the foulee. A close second was the pin and shoulder. There weren't many experienced players that would fall for this one. And if they did, they usually weren't inclined to let their opponent live to hear the final whistle. It should be new to Turki, though. Benny skewered the Tunisian to the spot with a heel and bowled him over with a shoulder. Ordinarily Benny's shoulder wouldn't have budged this chap more than a few inches, but when one of your feet is pinned to the spot, you go over like a sack of spuds.

Benny hared around the gym through to the building site. The pickup skidded to a halt behind him, showering gravel over the back of his head. This was cutting it a bit fine. At least he had the satisfaction of knowing that he'd bought the little Tunisian a minute to get over the wall. Because, in all likelihood, he was never going to see Omar again.

Unless, of course, the eejit was just standing there looking up at the wall. Which, amazingly enough, he was.

"Omar!" gasped Benny. "What in the name of God . . . ?"

Omar turned around, his face small and scared. "Binny *Khouya*. *Mafi* K-two boil up hot beefy Bovril."

Translation: No mountain. The mud hill was gone. Gama had obviously decided that no more cross-boundary friendships were going to develop. And by the thunderstruck look on Omar's face, he must've done it since the Ben Alis decided to take up residence in the village. Benny tried to think, but everything was closing in on him. He could feel the shadows of his pursuers on his neck. Omar was terrified. Grace was crying. How could you contain this? If they caught Omar, what would they do to him?

Benny did what came naturally. He jumped for the lip of the wall. Good takeoff . . . bad impact. He whacked into the concrete, cracking his hip painfully, but he got an elbow over. Mohamed was around the corner now. His voice was clear, not bouncing off anything.

This was Benny's chance. He had a legitimate opportunity to slide back down to earth. No one could say he hadn't made a Trojan effort for his friend. Benny caught sight of Kaheena's face from under Omar's armpit. He pulled himself over the top.

"Come on," he said, reaching down a hand. "Give me the sprog! *Feesa!*"

Omar was already stepping out of the homemade baby carrier.

Oh no! Don't throw her! Omar lobbed the wriggling package upward. It was more of a heft, really. After all, this girl was nine years old. Benny caught the knotted sleeves, the weight nearly dragging him off the wall. A clatter of blue jumpsuits was descending on them. Benny had no doubt that if Mohamed and his cronies did get hold of him, they'd have to be pulled off with stun guns. He leaned back, trying to counterbalance Kaheena's weight with his own. She was just sort of slumped there, a big lump of dead weight. It was like trying to heave a sack of potatoes with one hand.

"Hold on, ma'am," said Omar. "Help is on the way."

Benny knew Omar couldn't make it. He hadn't the legs on him. They were done for. Unless the Tunisian explained the concept of a leg up to Grace in about half a second. Omar did better. As gently as possible, he maneuvered the Scottish girl onto all fours by the wall, then he stepped up on her back and climbed over the top. What a gentleman!

Omar grabbed Kaheena just as Benny's knuckles were about to pop. They wrestled her onto the lip, draping her there like a side of beef. Things were hotting up below. Mohamed had intercepted Grace before she could join them. She was bawling and struggling, her hands bouncing off his chest. Samir was roaring up at the boys in Arabic. His face was flushed with rage. Gama's boys were hurling themselves at the wall, but long months of sly snoozes and cheap cigarettes had taken their toll. They bounced back like flies off a windshield. Mohamed handed Grace to Samir. He was going to try himself.

"Walahi," breathed Omar.

He dropped down to the outside world. Benny tipped Kaheena over and braced himself against the sudden jerk. But how effectively can you brace yourself on the top of a wall? The two of them went down in a heap, with not even a turkey to break their fall. Luckily they avoided any rocky outcrops, thumping into a soft bed of sand. Omar had Kaheena around his neck before Benny was even on his feet. He reached into some spiky scrub and wheeled out the moped.

"Inshallah," he prayed, swinging a leg over the block of velour and foam that masqueraded as a saddle.

Gama was groaning his way over the wall. His elbows were up now, and the top half of his head. It wasn't a happy half. The bike kick-started first time.

"Al-hamdu li'llah!" exulted Omar, revving the sleep out of the moped.

"Binny!" he shouted. *"Feesa!"*

"Emshee," coughed Benny. "Go on, will ye!"

Omar revved, but held the bike with the brake. Like a dog on a leash.

"Mafi go!" he nodded at the wall. *"Shuf."*

Benny looked. Mohamed was swinging his legs over now. Those humungous Docs looked ready to do serious damage. The bottom half of the guard's head was just as angry as the top half. "Angry" didn't even begin to cover it. He was roaring and spitting, and moments away from laying his hands on Benny's skinny neck.

"Benny Shaw!" he yelled.

That did it for Benny. Gama knew his name and where he lived. Time to make an exit. He could negotiate later. He jumped on the moped. Omar let off the brake the instant his friend's rear end touched the seat. They sped off across the desert, a ten-foot wave of dust arcing up in their wake.

Somehow, through all the clamor, Benny could hear

Grace crying. You're in for it now, boy, said the masks. And they were right. He'd never been in this much trouble in his life. Things were so bad that he wasn't even sure what the worst thing he'd done was.

Kaheena was staring back at him over her brother's shoulder. Her eyes didn't seem happy or sad, just open. Instead of getting the big, swelly heroic-type feeling that you'd think he'd get after saving a girl, Benny just wished he'd never clapped eyes on her. He buried his face in Omar's phosphate-soaked jacket, trying to find a bit of shelter.

13
THE DUKES OF HAZZARD

Benny would never forget the details of the next few days. They were just too shocking to slip your mind. They went into town on the bike. This really was a different world. The squalor went on and on.

Omar kept going, threading through the screaming and hubbub, past gray buildings and pungent stalls. Benny closed his eyes but the diesel fumes, spices, and chatter painted the picture in his head anyway.

Omar took a side road out of the market area. The buildings weren't as high now. Most of them weren't even finished. That didn't stop anyone occupying them. Families moved in the minute one story was ready. Then they hung out the washing upstairs or tied a TV antenna on to the red cinder blocks. The tarmac eventually gave up altogether, yielding to hard clay, dusty palm trees, and prickly pears.

Just when Benny thought his bones and cartilage were

turning to mush, Omar pulled the moped over. Benny fell off, wondering if his knees would ever click together again. They were on the outskirts of the town. A crowd of little schoolkids was trekking home to some distant village and a filthy toddler was dragging a sheep out of a ditch by the hind legs.

They had stopped in front of a garage about the size of a public toilet cubicle. There was a little hand pump outside for the moped mix. Someone had painted the Peugeot lion on the wall in drippy yellow emulsion. There was a fat fellow, presumably the owner, filling up a two-seater sofa outside the doorway. He wore a loose gray kaftan and thong sandals. Omar unhooked his sister and heaved her over to Benny.

"Binny," he said. "Don't move, don't even breathe."

Benny nodded, draping Kaheena's arms around his neck. For someone with such skinny legs, she weighed a ton.

Omar strolled up to the Man Mountain. "*Ya*, Ahmed," he called. "*Sh'nawalek?*"

Ahmed looked up from the big water pipe he was smoking. "Omar Ben Ali," he rumbled. "*Ena labes, sah-bee.*"

Benny sort of lost track of it after that, but it was obvious they were bargaining about something. They went through all the usual stages. First it was all very blasé.

Nobody was really interested. It was all just too boring. Then it went the other way. All roaring and gestures. At one stage Ahmed even made a grab for Omar's leg. But he never had a chance, and got a clip on the fingers for his trouble.

Inevitably they struck a deal. It was sealed with a meaty handshake and a round of cheek kissing. Omar's head looked like it had been slimed. Give me a written contract any day, thought Benny. Omar beckoned to him. He hurried over, skipping warily past the bloated proprietor. He needn't have bothered. Ahmed had already gone back to his pipe.

They went around the back and up a set of stone stairs. The whole place reminded Benny of a building site he used to horse around in at home. All bare boards and fittings. The walls weren't structurally complete yet. They'd got a few blocks up and then stopped. Steel rods jutted from the concrete, and the floor was bumpy and ridged with dried cement. So if you had no walls, then you obviously were not going to have any roof. There was only one room that was actually finished. Well, finished relative to the other rooms. There wasn't any door or plaster. Just blocks and Sheetrock. Omar clapped Benny on the shoulder.

Don't say it, thought Benny.

"Home sweet home," said Omar.

Omar managed to scrounge a few blankets from the whale downstairs, so the two of them sat out on the wall, feet dangling over the edge. Kaheena was sleeping in the back room.

"The Dukes of Hazzard," grinned Omar.

"Wha'?"

"The Dukes of Hazzard. Bo . . . Luke," he jerked a thumb toward the room. "Daisy."

"Three outlaws . . . Three eejits is more like."

"*Mafi* eejits. Binny, *khouya*."

"I know, I know. Bee Gees. Brothers. That's all very well and good, Omar, boy. But I have to go home."

"Pass?"

"Benny home sweet home—Marhaba village."

Omar nodded. "Sunrise on NBC."

"I should go now. It's dark already. Ma will be doing the nut altogether."

Omar got a bit sulky then. "*Emshee*, Binny."

"How can I? Sure I've no clue where I am . . . Binny Lost in Space."

Omar nodded toward Kaheena. "Married with children."

"I know. I know. You can't leave the young one."

Benny gazed out over the city, at the million dots of light floating below him. He imagined a shifty-eyed mugger in every doorway, just waiting to slice out some valuable organ. Even the cats around here were a bit scary when they gave you the eye.

"Maybe I'll hang on till the morning then. Sunrise."

"*Behee.*"

They raided Benny's gearbag. A few sandwiches. Some juice. Yogurt, apples, and a Mars bar. Fair play to you, Ma. Seeing as they didn't know when they'd eat again, the boys left half an apple for the morning. Kaheena wouldn't take anything. In fact, she seemed pretty disinterested in general. Benny remembered seeing Georgie like this after they'd put his arm in a cast. The gas had kept him all dopey for ages. Omar just stayed with her, tucking the blankets up under her chin and wiping her face down with Benny's hanky.

Benny sat on the blocks, trying to keep any bare flesh inside his blanket. Apparently they were having record heat this year so the mosquitoes were still breeding. He remembered what Grandad had said to him centuries ago, before they'd left Ireland: Africa is going to crack open your skull like an old dog with a legless crab. He understood that now. It was like people here didn't have childhoods. They hadn't the luxury of playing, or making mistakes, or sulking. You just had a hard life and that was about the size of it. And here he was, smack bang in the middle of all this living.

Benny was experiencing a new feeling. A bit like hunger, only lower down. It wasn't fear, he was used to that one. It seemed to him that all the stuff he used to worry about was so stupid. If Georgie got one sweet extra, he'd sulk. Or if Da wanted to watch the news, he'd flounce off. Benny realized what the feeling was. It was shame.

Then the rain started. Roadside coffee shops were emptied as the men hared inside like kicked dogs. Even Ahmed managed to winch himself out of the couch and shuffle indoors. Oh perfect, thought Benny. Just perfect.

Serves you right, said the masks.

Oh shut up, smart alecks, broadcast Benny.

He considered staying out there. Just let the rain batter him until he blended into the mud and flowed off down the drain. But the rain was too heavy. It whacked off the top of his head, hard enough to bruise. It seeped through the lining of his shorts. There's nothing like that squishy underpants feeling to get you up and moving.

The little room was fairly crowded with the three of them in it. Kaheena was looking pretty pasty.

"*Mush behee*," said Omar. "I gotta bad feeling about this."

Benny was trying to wring out his shorts. "Well, at least it can't get any worse." Imagine saying that. The dopey eejit!

Benny had just nodded off in the corner when Kaheena started crying. First he thought he was still in his dream and Jessica was sobbing over his open coffin. He looked nice too. All angelic and manly. There wasn't even any sign of the cowlick. Then his ma's mouth opened wider and wider. It was the saddest face he had ever seen. Her tears spurted out like the Old Spice wave, drumming off the sides of his pine casket. He tried to tell her to stop. It was okay. He wasn't dead! But she wasn't listening. Jessica Shaw was inconsolable. Her wailing was straight out of *Riders to the Sea*. Stop it, will you, Ma, he shouted, I'm all right. But suddenly he knew that she wasn't crying over him. It was her masks. He'd lost the masks. Pat Shaw gave him a wink. We're going to try harder with Georgie, he whispered conspiratorially. It's our last chance. If we break him, they won't give us another one.

"Binny! *Shuf*."

He opened his eyes. Kaheena was breaking her vow of silence. Not only that, but she was making up for all the years of saying nothing. The poor girl was hysterical. Screaming and waving terrified hands in front of her face. Omar hung on to her thin frame, muttering into her ear. It was no use.

Omar's face was grim. "Drugs, Binny. *Mush behee*. No good."

What could Benny do but nod and help? He wrapped his blanket around Kaheena's wasted legs, trying to rub some warmth into them. Omar stroked her lank hair and kissed her forehead. It was easy to guess what nightmare her tortured brain was reliving. That train was bearing down on her family, crashing into their pickup over and over again.

Omar was crying now. Crying with helplessness and frustration. Not everything could be cured with a hug and a joke. Benny found himself getting all emotional too. Big blubbery tears popped out of his eyes and nose.

It seemed to go on forever. Kaheena would be grand for a while, sort of dreaming with her eyes open. Then a spasm would hit her and the howling would begin again. Her body bucked and convulsed like she was trying to fly or something. And what could the two boys do about it? The only first-aid type stuff they knew came from *Baywatch*.

How in the name of God had he ended up here, Benny asked himself. From beside a cozy fire in Ireland to this hellhole. Omar's sister might die or anything. Coming off these drugs could drive her permanently out of her skull. And what would that make them? Murderers? Benny shuddered. Shut up, he told himself. What's the point in thinking that way? You'll be home tomorrow. Home tomorrow.

After a couple of hours, the rain started running down the inside of the walls. They found a high spot on the uneven floor and perched up on it. Whatever cowboys had built this place must've used a bad mix, because the floor was starting to dissolve into limey slush. They backed into a raised corner, draping Kaheena across their laps. All they could do was wait.

Four hours later the moment came. The one his Ma was always on about with her childbirth yarns. That second that made all the hassle sort of bearable. Benny wouldn't have believed it. Nothing was worth this. There was even a rat sharing the room with them now, for God's sake. What could possibly happen to take away the sting of that? Now, you're probably thinking: the rain stops, the sun peeks over the horizon. The ma and da rush in and embrace their son. They pledge their love and decide to adopt the Ben Alis. Well, no. Not exactly. The rain was still pelting down, threatening to dissolve their shelter. The rat was still twitching away nervously, his wet fur giving him a punky look. But just before dawn, Kaheena's brow smoothed out, right after a real bone shaker of a spasm. Omar mopped off her face with Benny's drenched hanky.

"*Sh'nawalek*, Kaheena?" he said, just talking. Not expecting an answer or anything. He'd been jabbering away all night.

"*Ena labes*," said Kaheena, her voice all croaky.

Omar nearly dropped her head with the shock. And from somewhere inside him, he found another well of tears.

"Kaheena," he wept, hugging her even closer.

Kaheena reached up a shaky arm and pawed his head. "*Shouya, shouya*, Omar. *Shouya, shouya*."

And for that second Benny forgot all about what was happening to him. Even more surprising, he forgot what was going to happen tomorrow when Mohamed Gama caught sight of him coming through the village gates. Well, who cared? They could all go jump in a lake. He'd made the right decision, and nobody who could see these two hanging off each other would be able to argue with him.

There was no sign of the rain easing off or the rat leaving. But at this stage the little rodent was like one of the gang. Kaheena was obviously all talked out for the night and had conked out on her brother's lap. What else was there to do but sleep? So they did. But it was one of those surface sleeps where you know exactly what's going on around you. Omar was worried that Kaheena might start talking again. Benny was concerned that their little rat buddy might call his friends.

Morning brought a grim sort of daylight. And that was about it. The deluge had dribbled out temporarily but there were a heap of broody looking clouds floating about. They were still saturated. Plus they were all starving. At least the rat was gone. Benny woke up feeling like a wet toilet roll.

Omar was in good form, though.

"Asslama, sahbee," he grinned, punching his buddy on the arm. The contact sounded like steak being slapped on a board.

"Asslama, Smiley." Benny shook some water from his ears.

"Shuf, Binny."

Benny looked. Kaheena was sitting up in the corner. She was still looking a bit on the wild side, but at least there was no fit-throwing.

"Howza goin' there, Kaheena? Ah . . . *Asslama.*"

Kaheena sort of nodded dreamily. Harmony would love this one. An apprentice hippie.

"Hey, Omar. I'm starvin', boy. Anything left to eat?"

"Eat? Sunshine breakfast?"

"That's it. *Na'am!*"

Omar fished out the browned apple-half from the gearbag. Kaheena squealed when she saw it.

Benny sighed. "Ah, go on. Give it to the youngster."

Omar did. She sucked it to death. The sight of apple juice trickling down the little girl's chin didn't do anything for the two lads' gurgling stomachs.

"Hey, Omar?"

"*Na'am.*"

"Any chance Fat Boy below there might give us a bit of grub?"

"Pass."

"Ah . . . Ahmed?"

"*Na'am.*"

"Ah . . . cornflakes. Hovis. Mars bar."

"Work, rest, and play?"

"*Na'am.* Yeah."

Omar nodded his head, droplets flying from his hair. "*Na'am.* Tomorrow, tomorrow, I love you tomorrow."

"Oh, I get it. No work, no dosh. *Mush behee*, Omar boy. I'm hungry now."

Omar shrugged. "*Mafi* dinars."

The word *dinars* sparked Benny's memory. He'd been thinking in Irish money. The mention of Tunisian currency reminded him of Da's little parting gift.

"Hold on there now a sec! Wait'll we see what I've got here."

Benny peeled himself out of the sagging cement and rooted around in his jacket. Suddenly he was freezing. He must've warmed up his own little mud puddle overnight. Benny tried to stop his hands shaking long enough to get them into his pockets. How fast did Tunisian money decompose, he wondered? Would the vendors accept a handful of inky pulp? He found it. Wet and soggy but still recognizable.

"*Voilà!*" he crowed, laying the note on his palm like a slice of bacon. Twenty dinars. God bless you, Pat Shaw.

Omar could only gawk. It wasn't often a young fellow like him would be looking at this sort of denomination.

"*Al-hamdu li'llah!*" he breathed.

"You can sing it," grinned Benny, the thought of food giving him a lift. Omar rapidly got over being awestruck. He hoisted Kaheena up around his neck. She was speaking a bit now, and playing with her brother's face. They descended the slippery stairs carefully. There was a layer of mud slopped over everything. Cats were picking their way along walls, trying to stay dry. Omar's new boss and landlord was perched on a fertilizer bag that covered his couch. He barely looked up from his pipe. He'd hardly be doing a whole heap of business in this weather. So there was no objection to Omar heading off.

It was a testament to the little Tunisian's skill as a mechanic that the battered old moped started up at all. But it did, spewing stringy dollops of sooty water out of the exhaust.

"*Al-hamdu li'llah,*" muttered Benny, before Omar could say it.

"*Al-hamdu li'llah,*" echoed Kaheena. Another baby step on her voyage back to the land of the living.

They mounted up, the saddle foam depositing its cache of dirty water down their thighs. Kaheena reached over her brother, grasping Benny's nose with inquisitive fingers.

"Stop, will ye?" grinned Benny.

He would never tell, he decided. He would never tell anybody where they were. Kaheena was better off on the back of some old bike than strapped to a hospital bed. Good intentions or not, the results spoke for themselves. She poked a finger up his nose.

"Ah here! I'm serious now. Give that up!" As if a girl who's been drugged and restrained for three years is going to worry about a little Irish chap being stern with her.

So they motored on to the French market. None of the other drivers bothered to try and avoid splashing them.

There were a couple of Gardes Nationale up ahead lounging on BMW bikes. These were about the coolest crowd in town. Real SS-looking uniforms with shiny knee boots. They were armed too: holstered handguns hanging off their hips, and sometimes even some sort of machine gun. Benny felt the muscles in Omar's back tense. Of course! The police were more than likely looking for the whole lot of them by now. They probably had those photofit things and everything. Two boys and a small girl, wanted for questioning in connection with a whole heap of stuff.

They needn't have bothered worrying. There was that

much muck on the three of them that it looked like the moped was being ridden by the Blob. The two guards weren't killing themselves, anyway. One more orphan running around Sfax wasn't going to destroy any delicate ecosystem. Anyway, to keep an eye on the traffic they might have to get their boots dirty.

Omar whipped past, running a red light in the process. A moped stopping at the traffic lights would only attract attention.

The whole idea was a bit stupid, really. Benny didn't actually know where they were headed or he might have voiced a complaint. Then again, cold and hungry runaway that he was, he might not.

I mean, where were they going? The French market. And where was all the fresh produce for Marhaba village acquired? Three guesses. This was the day that the smiling vendors washed off all the stock and hiked up the prices three hundred percent. So it was inevitable that they were going to be spotted. So much for the inbred cunning of young lads.

Omar parked beside a tethered goat and barged into the market like he owned the place. Which, with twenty dinars, he more or less did. Benny slunk along behind him, trying to look inconspicuous. Still, with the amount of mud on him, he could have kissed his Ma and she'd never have recognized him.

Food was the first order of the day. Omar hitched Kaheena up around his middle and made for a little stall. The proprietor knew Omar and didn't seem too thrilled to see him. Until the little Tunisian casually let the edge of his twenty dinar note show through his fingers. And then, sure, they were best buddies. The boys bought fresh baguettes, soft white cheese, orange juice, and a big bar of dark chocolate. And that only set them back about two dinars.

Omar unhooked Kaheena, propping her up against a pillar. He broke off a square of chocolate for her to suck. Then the two boys took care of themselves. They tore open the bread and squeezed cheese into it through a crack in the foil. The hot dough reacted with the cheese to form a gooey mush. It was deadly. The two boys kept going, poking chocolate squares down the center of the rolls. This way you got your three basic texture groups: crunchy, chewy, and sloppy.

Eighteen inches later they were finished. For the first time in ages Benny felt a bit relaxed. He might be a wet, filthy runaway, but at least he was full. Omar burped. A mammoth explosion that ballooned his cheeks. You couldn't let something like that go unanswered. Benny leaned his head back to get the maximum airflow down the gullet. He took a deep breath and rolled his stomach like a belly dancer. The resultant belch would have cracked an urn at twenty yards.

"Mabrook," said Omar sincerely. "Congratulations and celebrations."

Kaheena burped too. It was weak and girly, but at least she was making the effort.

One little sunbeam battled its way through the cloud cover and, for a second, Benny felt good. Then he began to notice things. His feet were numb. And the dirt and phosphate were burning into his nooks and crannies. Funny thing was, his fingers were clean. They'd been dirty before their meal. There was a public loo across the way.

"Right, I'm going for a wash before you drop me out to the Marhaba."

"Wash?"

"Ah . . . Relax in a Radox bath."

Omar nodded. "Wash that man right outta my hair."

"Yeah, whatever." He wiggled his fingers. "*Cinq* minutes, okay?"

"Okily dokily."

When he came back he found that Omar had been busy spending a few more bob. Two multicolored mattresses were hanging off the back fender, rolled and tied like those modern bales of hay. A goat was having a sly chew. Omar gave the unfortunate animal a kick that would've earned a two-point conversion in Lansdowne Road.

"*Ya*, Benny," he shouted, pummelling the mattresses to demonstrate their spring. "*Shuf.*"

"Yeah. I see them. Couldn't you find anything a bit colorful?"

"All the colors in the rainbow," sang Omar, the simple purchase cheering him up no end. He hugged his sister tightly, finger-combing her hair behind her ears.

There were a couple of silicon guns sticking out of the legs of Omar's tracksuit. Looked like he'd be sealing up a few leaks above the Fat Man's shop.

"Home sweet home," said Benny, nodding at the mastic.

"*Na'am, khouya,*" replied the Tunisian, pulling his sister close. "Omar. Kaheena. Home sweet home."

"Swee-ome," mumbled Kaheena.

The little fellow was really determined to make a go of it. And bit by bit he'd make that building site they were squatting in more like a home. Benny had no doubt of it.

"Binny ride into the sunset?"

Benny nodded. "Yep. You just drop me at the main road."

"Okeydokey."

Getting on the bike was a bit trickier this time. Benny hooked his arms through the baling twine tying the mattresses together. At least if he went off the back there'd be a bit of a soft landing before the rest of the traffic ran over him. This was real lunatic-type behavior. Their center of gravity was so far back at this stage that if a couple of flies tried to land on the mattresses, they'd have the whole lot of them on their ears. But not to worry, Omar compensated by hanging two bags of shopping on the handlebars.

Abdel Bakri was in a foul mood. Here he was, one of Mohamed Gama's top boys, doing Saturday shopping for a crowd of females! The shame of it. Like he had nothing else to do but pick up chicken wings for that American woman!

"Well?" said the chicken man (in Arabic, of course).

"Have you any wings?" said Abdel, trying to sound as if the wrong answer meant death.

The chicken man licked his bare gums. "Not personally, no," he said.

"What?"

"Of course I have wings! *Beleed!* It's a chicken shop!"

"Give me half a kilo then," pouted Abdel.

Abdel drew his walkie-talkie like a cowboy pulling his six-shooter. Now this was true style. No one could doubt his stature when they saw him talking into one of these. Those kids over by the baker's, for instance. Hopefully they'd come this way and he could start speaking in code. A few Bravo Ones and Tango Sevens should have them gasping all the way back to whatever hovel they crawled out of.

Abdel paused. Two boys and a crippled girl. A little light bulb was trying to flash on in his head. Two boys and a crippled girl. What was it? Something about a . . .

Walahi! Abdel remembered! The Irish boy, Binny something. Mohamed's pet hate. Abdel fumbled with the dials on his Motorola. This would get him squash-court detail for sure. The walkie-talkie came alive with a burst of static.

"*Uskut!*" Abdel hissed, skipping behind a pillar. "Bravo One?"

Hiss . . . crackle . . .

"Bravo One? This is Abdel."

Hiss . . . crackle . . . "This is Bravo One."

Abdel cheered silently. Good. "*Ya*, Husni . . ."

"This is Bravo One."

"Husni. It's me, Abdel."

"This is Bravo One. Identify yourself."

"Husni . . ." Abdel fumed silently. His brother Husni was getting a bit carried away with radio protocol.

"Bravo One, this is Tango Seven, over."

"Receiving you, Tango Seven. What is your difficulty?"

"I don't actually have a difficulty . . ."

"No difficulty! This frequency is to be kept clear for emergencies."

"It is an emergency!"

"But you specifically said——"

"Husni. I am going to kick you very hard when I return."

"Threatening me will not change regulations."

"And so will Mohamed Gama."

"I don't think . . ." Husni paused. "Gama?"

"Yes!" screeched Abdel triumphantly. "I have the boy. The Irish boy. He's right here in front of me."

"If you could just wait a moment, Tango . . . Abdel."

"Al-hamdu li'llah," breathed Abdel.

When the chicken man returned, his customer was gone. He spotted the young man dodging in and out of the pillars. Crazy, no doubt. There were many crazy people in Sfax. The sunshine and phosphate residue was bleaching their brains. The chicken man sighed. He'd be back. They all came back. Everybody had to eat chicken.

The phone rang. Pat Shaw had it to his ear before the tone had faded. "Yeah," he said. "Yeah. Okay. I'm on my way."

"Well?" pleaded Jessica, her face a washed-out mask of tears.

"They've spotted them. At the French market. One of the guards is on their tail."

"Oh, thank God," sighed Jessie, pulling Georgie to her chest. "Thank God."

Stuart Taft got up from the couch. "I'll drive."

"Right so, Stuart. Come on."

"I'm going too," said Grace. She'd been there since Benny went over the wall.

"Ah here," said Pat, "why don't we just sell tickets?"

"Pat!"

"I haven't time for this, Jessie!"

But Grace was adamant. Like she'd been about not going home. "I'm going," she repeated. "Benny likes me."

"Oh, all right! Everybody into the jeep."

The rain was starting again. It lashed down on them. Parts of the road were still flooded. It didn't seem to bother Omar, though. He just burst on like the muddy water wasn't even there. 'Course the mattresses weighed a ton by now. Benny could feel the baling twine cutting into his shoulders. Any minute now and they'd all be face down in the muck.

Kaheena was looking over her brother's shoulder. Her nose was running a bit. "Inny," she said.

"Don't you start!"

"Inny," repeated Kaheena.

"It's Binny! I mean Benny." God Almighty! Binny was bad enough. But Inny!

"Binny," smiled Kaheena.

"Ah, close enough," sighed Benny. He lifted the corner of Omar's tracksuit and wiped the girl's nose.

Omar elbowed him. "R-S," he hissed.

"What?"

"R-S. *Shuf.*"

Benny remembered. R-S were the first two letters of foreign business license plates. All the EuroGas plates were R-S. Benny squinted through the sheets of rain. White Discovery.

"*Mafi mushkela*, Omar. Could be anyone. Just keep her steady."

"Aye aye, cap'n."

Whoever it was, was bursting along at a fair old whack. Throwing up twin waves in his wake. We're nabbed, thought Benny. Whoever's driving that is looking for us. How could they have known, though? He twisted his head around, trying not to bat the other two with the mattresses. There was an R-S pickup trailing them too. Benny grabbed Omar's shoulder.

"Warp speed," he shouted, through gobfuls of acrid water.

The little Tunisian slapped a few dials and managed to drag a good burst out of his bike. 'Course the rain fell even harder now. It was like someone emptying a never-ending bucket right over their heads. The Discovery driver spotted them. He jammed on the brakes, aquaplaning wildly across the slick surface. Too late. The little bike zipped past. Benny caught a look at the man behind the wheel. It was Mohamed Gama. He was not a happy chappie.

"Binny," shouted Omar. "Bogies at two o'clock."

This was a bit much. It wasn't as if they were armed robbers or anything. There was another Discovery bearing down at them. And this one was on the wrong side of the road! Either your man was an utter maniac altogether or he was having a flashback to UK driving. They were trapped! Gama behind and this new guy in front.

"*Walahi,*" yelled Omar. "No retreat, no surrender."

Kaheena was bawling now. The tears dribbled from her eyes and nose, mingling with the rain rivulets. They were through Tyna now, there weren't even any buildings to hide behind. Just the railway track on one side and a narrow spit leading down to the Mediterranean on the other. Kaheena saw the tracks and went ballistic. Omar leaned into her, fighting to keep them upright. They slewed in the puddles, losing traction for a second.

The Discovery facing them switched on its high beams, trying to flash them down.

There was only one way for them to go. Omar skidded on to a dirt path, cutting down through the olive groves. Kaheena calmed. At least they were heading away from the tracks. The last thing Benny saw, before he started vibrating like a kid working a jackhammer, was his father's face in the windshield of the oncoming Discovery.

For some reason that made him cry like a baby.

And still the rain hammered them. Beating them down with a million stingy darts. It flooded the olive groves, creeping up the sides of the clay mounds that acted as fences. It crept in under the topsoil, raising it like scum in a well. Weak roots were dragged out. Tethered animals drowned, squealing for help. It was a hell of a lot of water.

"Stop, Omar!" cried Benny. "Give it up, will you? Red light!"

"*Mafi* red light," grunted his friend. "Omar, Kaheena ride off into the sunset."

The end, when it came, hit them like a ton of bricks. One farmer had used an old door as part of his fence. The door, fair play to it, had exceeded its design parameters and kept several thousand liters of muck and assorted plants at bay for nearly eight hours. But this last deluge was too much. As the moped whizzed by, the wood sighed, cracked, and splintered. The door went, and with it the whole fence. The entire enclosure and its contents gushed out toward the ocean. It was a fantastic sight to see—a seemingly intact field riding on the torrents.

Benny didn't see it. Neither did Omar. The flood scooped them up and tried to pop them through the prickly-pear hedge.

Try to imagine how they were feeling. Two young lads and a disturbed girl, shredded through the sharp teeth of grabbing trees. They flailed in the mesh of branches like dolphins in a net. Dekaliters of water sluiced between them. Clouds of furious steam rose hissing from the bike's tank. Benny couldn't scream. He couldn't see. Bubbles were popping in his eyes. Missiles were bouncing off his body and head. Omar was all twisted around; somehow they were face-to-face. They held on to each other, sandwiching Kaheena between them.

The bike jerked forward, shotgunning through the trees' pawlike flowers. In an instant it was gone, steaming and spinning into the currents. Benny dragged Omar into a headlock. Kaheena's face was crushed against his chest.

C'mon, Da, thought Benny. C'mon, will ye.

Only his mattress backpack was keeping their heads above water. The covers had split and the foam was disintegrating over his shoulders.

Then something hit them! It bashed into Benny's ribs, winding him instantly. He felt the pinpricks of broken wood. The door panel spun and whacked Omar in the face. Instinctively they let go, hands flying to their wounds. Benny gasped for air, but all he got was gritty water. The current was driving a wedge between them. Omar's nose was bleeding. A pink trail ran out behind him. He grabbed Benny's shirt.

"Kaheena," he gurgled.

Benny could only grope blindly. Come on, Da!

Benny managed half a breath. The meager gasp of oxygen fortified him. He scrabbled his hands around Kaheena's waist, twining his fingers together. They were all locked together now. A human chain, with Benny hooked to the mattress which was jammed onto the prickly branches. But there was a weak link in the chain: the knots on the jumpsuit holding Kaheena to Omar that were never meant to withstand this sort of stress.

The top one went! The two boys couldn't even see what was happening. Blood, water, and debris swirled around them, gagging them, blinding them. Omar flipped backward, his hand ripping free from Benny's collar. The Irish boy felt the snap of his mother's chain being torn off his neck.

"C'mon, Da," screamed Benny. "Come on, will ye?"

Omar was lolling backwards, a rag doll gripped by the power of the flood. His face was red with blood.

"Omar!" screamed Benny, but he couldn't even hear himself. "Omar! Hang on."

Kaheena was bucking in his arms, he could feel her sharp bones scraping across his chest.

"Da! Da!"

The jumpsuit was slipping. Down Omar's legs, only the crook of his knee holding it up. Omar was still fighting, boxing the deluge like an opponent. Benny wanted to reach out, but it meant letting go of Kaheena. Maybe he could just use one hand. Just for a second. Just a quick grab.

Omar read his mind.

"*Laa, sahbee!*" he spat. "*Mafi* helping hand! Kaheena nine one one!"

"Omar! Please."

Somehow in all that turbulence they locked eyes.

"Binny Bee Gee," said Omar, trying to flash that stupid grin of his.

The water pulsed and he was gone. Ripped right out of the jumpsuit. Benny screamed, wrapping arms and legs around Kaheena. There was no drawn-out final scene, like in the movies. No solitary hand wiggling above the waves. Just suddenly there was no more Omar.

Benny heard a rip. The mattresses slipped another notch. They were holding on by strands now. Once the trees gave up their prickly hold, the saturated foam would sink them like a rock.

Another rip. The water dragged at their feet with greedy fingers. Benny could feel the baling twine biting into his armpits. Kaheena sagged in his arms like a bag of coal.

"Da! C'mon! I'm sorry."

And then Da came. Strong hands grabbed Benny and hauled him out through the bushes. He could see his blood being instantly diluted and whisked away. Those battered legs didn't feel like his. Or maybe like his in a dream. Pat Shaw's face came into view.

"Benny!"

"Da."

"Hang on, boy."

Benny did, never loosening his viselike grip on Kaheena. He saw breath bubbles bursting on her lips and she sneezed a noseful of water on his jacket. Thank God! Something big and blue flashed past them, plunging into the torrents. It was Mohamed Gama. Going after Omar. He burst through the prickly pears like they weren't there.

Da had them out on the path now. Away from the direct flow. The rest of them were waiting by the Land Rover, up to their knees in mud. Da dumped Benny and Kaheena on the hood. They huddled together, shivering. Benny couldn't let go. Omar had told him not to.

Everyone gathered around, rubbing the saturated pair with coats and blankets.

"They're all right," said Pat. He sounded like he was telling himself. "They're all right!"

Jessica could only sob and hug the sopping bundle of twigs and bruises that was her eldest son. Benny opened his eyes slowly, not trusting the water to leave him alone.

"Georgie?" he chattered. "Where's Georgie?"

His brother had been relegated to the back seat. Out of the way.

"Georgie?"

Showing agility for once in his life, George scrambled over the seats, through the window and onto the hood. Pat and Jessie had no clue what was going on here. Benny had never asked for Georgie. Never.

"You all right, Benny?" sniffed George. Real tears this time. No dramatics.

Benny flapped an arm at his brother. George reared back instinctively, expecting a puck, but it wasn't that kind of gesture. He knelt down, peering in over the Tunisian girl's head.

"What is it, Benny? What's wrong?"

Benny coughed, water plopping out over his chin. "I'm sorry, Georgie boy. I'm sorry. I understand it all now. I'm sorry."

It was like the end of a Lassie film or something. They nearly caused another flood with all the bawling that went on. Even Talal Khayssi, who'd been hanging around the other vehicle, got a bit sniffly.

Pat Shaw noticed Gama emerging sodden from the flood plain. The bulky guard shook his head silently. Pat sighed. No more than he'd expected.

"Right, let's go," he said gruffly. "Get this fellow to the clinic."

Mohamed Gama pried Kaheena from Benny's grip and folded her into his huge arms.

270

"Hold on there now . . ." began Pat, but Jessica put a hand on his arm, and it calmed him, as it always did.

"Let them off, Pat. She's one of their own. They'll look after her."

Pat nodded. It made sense, he supposed. He wasn't thinking very clearly at the moment. All these emotions were bouncing around inside his head. The strongest of all was dread. A cold dread of the moment when he would have to tell Benny that his buddy had been lost in the flood.

14

LOOSE ENDS

Grace and Benny were sitting up on the wall. Grace shielded her eyes with a palm.

"So where is it, then?"

Benny pointed at the mishmashed lump of plastic, brick, and tree. "See there. By the turkey."

"Oh, yeah. The flood really did a number on that didn't it?"

Benny sighed. "Yeah. Not to mention Gama and his cronies. It was a nifty little place too."

He had "the feeling" again. Like fear and nervousness rolled together. One of those emotions where you had to pause to think what was wrong with you. Some part of his brain was thinking about Omar.

"Look," said Grace.

An old man with a donkey and cart was picking through the remains of Omar's house. This was the saddest excuse for a donkey you were ever likely to see. The old fellow was raking through the wreckage with a broom handle.

Benny tensed. He wanted to shoo the man off. It was like grave robbing or something.

"God love that poor man," said Grace. "Rooting around in rubbish for a living."

"Yeah. God help him."

They sat quietly for a minute, drumming their heels on the concrete, watching the human scavenger load up his cart with semi-valuable rubbish. It took him all of ten minutes to strip Omar's shack to the bones. As an afterthought he whacked the turkey with his broom handle and slung it on the pile too. Benny would miss that turkey. But he would always carry a piece of its brother inside him.

Grace kicked his ankle. "Here, I've something for you."

"Wha'? Something for me! Go on out of that!"

Grace was embarrassed. She swung her hair forward to hide a crimson blush. "Sort of an early Christmas present. Here . . . look."

She handed him a little pink box with gold Arabic writing. There was a weird silver pendant thing inside.

"Oh . . . it's a . . ." What the hell was it?

"Half a heart."

"Oh, yeah. Look at that." There were letters carved into it. ST . . . and under that END.

"Ah . . . Saint End. Lovely. He's the patron saint of hurlers or something, is he?"

"No, you moron. It's the second half of BEST FRIEND." She pulled out a matching pendant from under her T-shirt. "I've got the other bit, look."

"Oh, righto." Benny ran his thumb across the letters. This, without doubt, was the single dopiest thing he had ever seen. If the boys at home heard about this, they'd burst their britches laughing.

Grace was peeping out from under her bangs, waiting for some sort of reaction.

"Thanks very much."

"Welcome."

That wouldn't do it, though. "Thanks" was a real neutral sort of word. I mean, you thanked a teacher for giving you back your own homework. So what did you say when a girl gave you a present? It wasn't like getting something from Ma and Da. They expected you to complain. Grace would be hoping for something nice. Should he just tell the truth? Say that this was the single tackiest piece of merchandise he'd ever laid eyes on?

The Scottish girl tucked a strand of blond hair behind her ear.

"This is great," said Benny, slipping the chain over his head. "The nicest present I've ever got. When I die they'll have to pry it off me chest." He paused. "Thanks, pal."

Grace giggled. Chuckle chuckle snort. "Bernard," she said, doing his mam again. "You are so eloquent. I may just allow you to bask in my popularity."

"Thanks, Your Majesty."

Grace dead armed him fondly. Right on the nerve too. Benny smiled. It felt good being nice just to be nice.

Family meeting. But it was different now. Benny was still sort of fond of Georgie since the flood. It was wearing off a bit, of course. Only natural.

"Bernard, George. We've a bit of news."

Here we go. "Not another move, is it, Mam?"

Jessica laughed as if that was a ridiculous idea. "No, no, Bernard. Nothing like that. This is good news— honestly. It's about Kaheena."

Benny felt his heart bursting off his ribs. Its pulse beat along every vein in his body. Everyone was looking at him to see what his reaction would be. There was a lot of that going on lately: seeing how Benny felt about things. Like losing Omar was going to drive him off the deep end or something. They did it slyly, though. He would turn around suddenly and catch everybody studiously not looking at him. "You've changed your minds?" he said.

Pat shook his head. "No, son. It just can't be done. The legal department doesn't want EuroGas employees getting into any wrangles down here."

"Yeah, but . . ."

"It's in my contract, Benny. I could be fired. Then there'd be no job and no Kaheena."

Benny knew that his da was right. But he'd promised Omar. He'd promised.

"It's all academic anyway."

"What d'you mean, Da?"

"Well, that young one has already been adopted."

Benny jumped to his feet. "What? You're joking me?"

"No, boy, I'm not."

"You said it took months just for the paperwork."

"I'd say there were a few backhanders involved. You know the way it goes in this country. A little baksheesh goes a long way."

Benny couldn't believe it. There went his extensive campaign to talk his parents around. He'd reckoned that Kaheena wouldn't be going anywhere. Sure, who'd want a nine-year-old well out of her cute stage? But now she was gone! He tried to calm himself.

"Well who, then? Who's got her?"

Jessica and Pat exchanged nervous glances.

"Come on, Da! Who is it?"

Pat Shaw took a deep breath . . . and told him.

Mohamed Gama was standing by the gatehouse.

"*Asslama*, Mohamed," said Benny, squinting against the glare from Gama's head.

The guard grunted. That was about as civil as he was going to get.

"Howzagoin'?"

Mohamed relented. He dropped his eyes to Benny's level. "How is what going?"

"Oh, I dunno. Everything. Life, the family, your kids."

"It is about Kaheena that you are asking?"

"S'pose," said Benny.

"Do not worry about her. She is well."

"How are the legs getting on?"

Mohamed's face changed. Nothing drastic, just a little softening around the eyes. "EuroGas has given us a wheelchair. The girl enjoys it very much."

"That's just great."

Gama sat and lit a cigarette, for him an act of almost unheard-of indiscipline. "Yesterday, she took two steps."

Benny grinned. "Two! She must like you, Mohamed, me bucko."

Gama shrugged. "It is my wife. She has always wanted . . ." He petered off.

"Yeah, I know what mothers are like. So, she saying anything yet, or what?"

The guard sat on the whitewashed step. He was still

taller than Benny. "No. No words yet. But I hope soon. She cries now not as much."

"Yeah, she's had a rough old time of it." He laid a hand on Gama's shoulder. "Listen, Mohamed, I know you tried saving Omar. I don't blame you or anything. Even though we were all, like, enemies and that."

If you didn't know Gama better, you'd swear he was nearly smiling. "*Shokran, Sidee* Binny." He locked eyes with the little Irish boy. "I believe that perhaps Omar Ben Ali did not wish to be caught. It would mean returning to a work farm. I believe that he likes his life the way it is."

"Was," corrected Benny.

Gama flicked his cigarette into the sand. Who cared about grammar in a foreign language?

"Any chance I could see her some time?"

The guard considered it. "In one month, ask me again. If my thoughts of you are all good, then yes."

"Aw here, Mohamed, that's blackmail."

Gama stood. Smoke break was over.

Benny scowled. "I'll do me best. I'm not making any promises, though."

"The choice is yours."

"*Asslama*, Mohamed," said Benny turning to leave. "I'll see you later."

"*Inshallah*," intoned the guard.

"Yep, *inshallah*."

Benny had only trudged off a few steps when Gama called his name. He turned to find something glittering in his face. At first Benny thought the guard was aiming his forehead shine straight at him. The way you do with a protractor on the classroom ceiling. But the twinkling object was spinning through the air. Mohamed's arms were by his sides, straight as an Irish dancer's. Benny snatched whatever it was before it could bonk him on the noggin. Its edges were familiar, even inside his closed fist. Slowly he peeled back his fingers. The monkey on his intestines yanked them like a flush chain. It was the drama mask pendant! The one Omar had snatched off his neck! What did this mean? He ran back to the gatehouse.

"Mohamed. What's the story?" he demanded. "Is Omar alive? Was this in the trees? Did you catch him visiting Kaheena? Tell us, will you?"

Gama said nothing.

Benny hopped up and down in frustration. "Ah, have a heart, Gama, ye eejit! Don't leave me hanging around like some gom! Tell me! Tell me!"

Mohamed, who had originally intended to take a bit of revenge on the Irish boy with this teasing clue, relented. "Samir Asaad found this in Kaheena's hand just before I collected her at the farm. He doesn't know how it got there." Mohamed paused, spearing Benny with a glare. "And neither do I."

Benny's gob flapped like saloon doors in the wind. "Righto! Gotcha!" He turned and raced back to the family unit, his stomach unkinking with every step.

"Da!" he roared, the gravelly rasp of a soon-to-be-broken voice coming out from under the squeaks. "Da! Da! Where are you? Family conference! Family conference!"

Mohamed Gama didn't know whether to grin or groan. He'd a feeling there'd be busy days ahead.

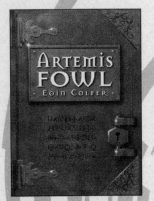
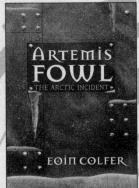
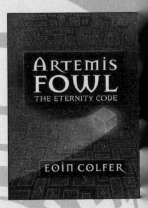
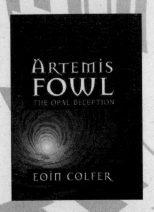
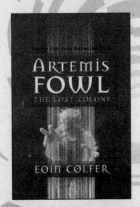
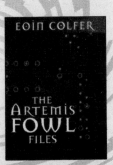